Chestnut Cove:

Love and Lessons

B. A. Howell

BA Howell, Publisher

Published by B. A. Howell

ISBN 978-1-7342536-2-7

This book is dedicated in loving memory to the author's parents, who always believed she could do anything she set her mind to and encouraged her to pursue her dreams. They also took her on vacation to the mountains instead of the beach on numerous occasions despite her occasional protestations. The mountains won her over.

Acknowledgements

The author would like to thank those who provided encouragement, support, suggestions, and assistance along the way, with special recognition to Allen, Dianne, Teddy, Jeri, Annie, and the Auburn Writers Circle, especially Larry, Cindy, Crystal, Robin, Jennifer, and Pete.

Editing by Annie Wiegel, AnneElizabethco.com

Cover design by Kristen Ingebretson, penmeetpaper.com

Cover photo by the author

This book is dedicated in loving memory to the author's parents, who always believed she could do anything she set her mind to and encouraged her to pursue her dreams. They also took her on vacation to the mountains instead of the beach on numerous occasions despite her occasional protestations. The mountains won her over.

Acknowledgements

The author would like to thank those who provided encouragement, support, suggestions, and assistance along the way, with special recognition to Allen, Dianne, Teddy, Jeri, Annie, and the Auburn Writers Circle, especially Larry, Cindy, Crystal, Robin, Jennifer, and Pete.

Editing by Annie Wiegel, AnneElizabethco.com

Cover design by Kristen Ingebretson, penmeetpaper.com

Cover photo by the author

Chestnut Cove Books

Chestnut Cove: Poseurs and Portraits, set in Spring 1979

Chestnut Cove: Love and Lessons, set in 1955-1956

Chestnut Cove: Belles and Balls, set in Summer/Fall 1979

Chestnut Cove: Devils and Daughters, set in 1958 (coming in September 2021)

Chestnut Cove: Odds and Inns, short stories set in the 1950s through 1960s (coming in the future)

Chestnut Cove: Inns and Outs, short stories set in the 1960s through 1970s (coming in the future)

Chestnut Cove: Revenge and Rapprochement, set in Fall 1979 (coming in the future)

Keep up with what's next with the characters of Chestnut Cove at bahowell.com

The Stuart Family and Their Friends

Kathryn McDougal Stuart: Owner of Chestnut Cove estate

Alistair Stuart: Kathryn's late husband; former owner of Chestnut Cove estate and several businesses in Elkford

John Stuart: Kathryn and Alistair's grandson and heir

Sandra Duncan: John's girlfriend

Matt Hunter: Kathryn's late sister's grandson; John's best friend

Jeanette Stevenson Stuart Hathaway: John's mother

Carlisle Stuart: John's late father; Jeanette's 1st husband

Winston Hathaway: Jeanette's 2nd husband; John's stepfather

Claudine: Winston's daughter from his first marriage

Millie Duncan: Kathryn's secretary; Sandra's mother

Greg Duncan: Sandra's brother

Earl Hunter: Matt's father

Lila: Kathryn's longtime cook and housekeeper

Mary: Lila's daughter; friend of John, Matt, and Sandra

Jonah Jones: Employee at Chestnut Cove; friend of John, Matt, and Sandra

Chapter 1

Tuesday, August 16, 1955

Sandra pulled away from her boyfriend and jumped up from the edge of the dock. Shuddering with a chill despite the warm night, she wrapped her arms around herself as she began to pace the wooden planking.

"Sandra, you're scaring me. Tell me what's wrong." John rubbed his hands down his face, baffled by her distress.

She stopped at the end of the dock, eyes on the shore across the lake. The fading daylight left the far side in little more than shapeless shadows. The girl took a couple of deep breaths and tried to speak, but her voice broke. "I need..." She sniffled and wiped at her eyes. "I need to tell you..."

When she lapsed into silence once more, John climbed to his feet and trailed after her, stopping close enough behind her to feel the heat emanating from her small frame. He placed his hands on her arms and pulled her back against his chest. "Sandra, just tell me what's bothering you. You know you can tell me anything. We've been sharing each other's secrets for a long time."

Her shoulders slumped, and she allowed her weight to lean into him, trying to gather strength from his embrace. Her sniffles became full-fledged sobs, and she turned to bury her face against his shoulder. When she could speak, she whispered, "I think I'm going to have a baby."

~~~

Wednesday, August 17, 1955

"My, you two must be the most diligent seniors at Elkford High School. The term hasn't begun and you two are already poking around the library." The woman's greeting caught John and Sandra off guard.

John tightened his grip on his girlfriend's hand. "We decided to research a few career choices today. We'll be so busy when school starts that we won't have much time for anything else. We thought we'd camp out in the reference department for an hour if that's OK."

"Of course, John. We'll be open until four o'clock today. Spend as much time as you want. Oh, and tell your grandmother the new encyclopedias she suggested we buy with part of her donation came in. I placed them on the shelves in reference just the other day." She pointed left to indicate the area in which he would find the new additions.

"I will. She'll be pleased." He stole a glance at Sandra. "We better get to work." He nodded to the librarian and led Sandra through the deserted county library toward an area where they would be out of sight. "Let's sit here." She nodded in silence and sat on a chair John pulled out from a worktable. "Are you all right?"

"Yes," she whispered. "We made the right choice to wait until after lunch. My stomach is still churning a little bit. I would have lost everything in it if we came here this morning." Her summer tan hid much of the paleness beneath. Breakfast for her had been light and short, remaining in place only long enough for her to excuse herself from the table without arousing suspicion and race on tiptoes to the bathroom. Fortunately, her light lunch fared better...so far. "Go find one of the legal books. I'll start looking for something in the first while you go back to find another one."

John checked the whereabouts of the librarian before pressing his lips to Sandra's. "I'll be right back." He slipped away to search for the books they wanted.

Twenty minutes later, they were engrossed in their research when a noise startled them. Across the room, the librarian struggled to raise a stuck window. John went to her aid and pushed it up.

"Thank you, John," said the woman. "I thought it was getting stuffy in here. You and Sandra should get a cross breeze at your table now." She returned to the desk, and John walked back across the room toward his girlfriend.

As he neared their table, he realized something was different. Sandra's pale complexion had a decidedly green cast to it, and she was panting softly. "What's wrong?" he whispered.

Her eyes darted to the window opposite the one John had helped open. He felt the air wafting across the table. It felt nice. Why would that adversely affect her? Then he caught a scent of fried fish. Peterson Fish House, located two doors down, must have a big group in for a late lunch. Sandra clamped her hand over her mouth. She jumped up and raced for the restroom. Her chair almost toppled backward, John just managing to grab it before it could crash to the floor.

His mind raced, trying to sort out what he could do to help her. The sudden movement had attracted the librarian's attention. They were lucky she couldn't see Sandra's coloring or realize the haste with which she raced toward the sanctity of the ladies' room. John couldn't risk the woman catching him trailing Sandra in there to check on her. He forced himself to return to his chair. Hidden behind low shelves of books, he wondered how long he would wait before throwing rationality away to follow her. Fortunately, the restrooms were located along the back wall behind some of the stacks, not near the door and front desk. Maybe if he crept along below the level of the shelves in the center of the room, he could sneak into the stacks to reach the back wall.

He was still plotting routes and excuses when he heard soft footsteps approaching. Sandra materialized from between the stacks, not looking significantly different than she had when they arrived. "Are you all right? Did the fish smell make you sick?" John whispered.

She slipped into her seat and squeezed his hand. "I'm better now. It hits fast and

then I actually feel better for a time. I washed my mouth out at the sink, but I'd like to get a soft drink when we leave here. They're supposed to help settle my stomach, too."

He slipped his arm around her and leaned his head against hers. "We can go now if you want. I don't want you trying to research our marriage options when you feel bad."

"No, it really is much better right now. I think I'm just going to need to get used to it. I know it goes away later." She pulled the book she had been reading toward her. "Let's get back to work."

As the clock ticked toward four, the dejected teens remained at their table. A stack of books, both those related to their cover story and the few they used for their true mission, surrounded them.

"It's no use, John. None of the surrounding states have less restrictive age limits." Her voice shuddered, the strain taking its toll.

"Then we'll convince our mothers to consent to us marrying as soon as possible. It's the responsible thing to do. They can't really object." Even as he said it, John wondered if his mother would see things that way. The discussion after Sandra's revelation the previous evening had been short and on point; they would marry as soon as possible.

Neither had any qualms about their future together other than its official start date. For now, that depended on either finding a place two seventeen-year-olds could wed, convincing their mothers to consent to an immediate marriage, or waiting until one or both came of age in the next few months. They didn't want to wait, but eloping didn't seem feasible based on their research.

Finding someone to create false identification for them hardly seemed realistic. Sandra had trouble convincing some people she was seventeen; no one would believe she was eighteen or older regardless of any fabricated papers they provided to an unknown, distant Justice of the Peace.

Sandra's sagging shoulders and drawn face showed her distress and exhaustion. John stood and collected the books they had used. Once he returned them to their proper locations, he hurried back to Sandra and held out his hand to her. "Let's get out of here. You need to rest. We can drive to the creek and sit and talk more, or you can sleep while I think of more options or how best to convince our mothers."

She stood, not bothering to respond otherwise, and slipped her hand into his. John said their goodbyes to the librarian as he led his love out of the building.

~~~

Thursday, August 18, 1955

The clock in the living room struck five, and John rolled over in bed. Another two hours before the sun rose. He managed little sleep the last two nights, and he held scant hope of getting more between now and dawn. Sandra's news had come as a shock, but his primary concern involved the amount of strain on her and how best to minimize it.

They had exhausted all reasonable avenues available to them and dismissed each in turn except the obvious one; they needed the consent of their mothers to marry as soon as possible. Both John and Sandra had lost their fathers years earlier. Sandra's died in battle near Salerno in 1943; John's succumbed in 1950 to complications from injuries sustained in 1944 when his bomber was shot down over Germany. That meant consent for marriage before they turned eighteen must come from their respective mothers.

He held some hope Millie Duncan would agree. She had known him since she became his grandmother's secretary seven years earlier. She seemed to like him, and she and his grandmother thought highly of one another. Besides, her daughter was the one who was pregnant. Society would not frown on the male Stuart heir the same way it would the pregnant, working-class daughter of a widowed secretary. However, society's opinion meant nothing to John. He loved Sandra, and he intended to marry her. He had already planned to do so once they finished high school, long before she became pregnant with his child.

He sat up and punched at his pillow before settling back on the bed again. Their real problem would be his mother. When he and Sandra transitioned from friends to a couple about two years ago, his mother began to belittle the girl at every turn. Jeanette Stevenson Stuart Hathaway wanted her only child to marry money, and the more, the better. Her first choice was her second husband's daughter, Claudine Hathaway. A year younger than John, Winston's daughter decided two years ago she wanted to move from Woodbury, where she lived with her mother and maternal grandparents, to Elkford so she could live with her father, stepmother, and stepbrother. It took little time to realize she did so because she had designs on John, which Jeanette and Winston encouraged at every opportunity. No, his mother would not be readily swayed to consent to an immediate marriage to Sandra.

John's mind turned to his real hope: Kathryn McDougal Stuart, his paternal grandmother and current owner of Chestnut Cove, the Stuart estate in the Appalachian Mountains, and the rest of the Stuart properties. While she would be disappointed in John for not showing more restraint, she thought a great deal of Sandra and made no secret of her satisfaction with a match between her only heir and the daughter of her secretary. She would be pleased with John for standing by the girl and insisting they do the right thing.

Moreover, Gramma Kate held the purse strings for Jeanette and Winston. They lived in a cottage on the Stuart estate at her expense, and she got him his current job at a bank in Elkford. Kathryn intimated on several occasions when Jeanette complained about something that their tenure on the Stuart estate could end once John left for college. He maintained a bedroom in the main house, much to Jeanette's chagrin. Jeanette and John had continued to live there after Carlisle, John's father, died until Jeanette married Winston a year later.

Upon their return from their honeymoon, they were shocked to learn Kathryn had moved Jeanette's things out of the big house into a cottage on the estate. However, John retained his room in the mansion along with receiving one in the cottage, and Kathryn decreed he could stay in either place at any time. Privately, Jeanette seethed at the interference, but she knew they could be kicked off the estate at her former mother-in-law's whim. With Winston fired from his ex-father-in-law's bank and the Hathaway family's fortune not nearly what Jeanette expected when she agreed to marry it, they had no recourse but to accept what Kathryn Stuart offered.

John abandoned any hope of more sleep, sat up, and swung his legs off the bed.

While he had always avoided the conflict between his mother and grandmother as best he could, for once he knew he would use it to his advantage if necessary to marry Sandra as soon as possible. Sandra deserved whatever support he could give her, and if that meant leveraging his grandmother's help, so be it. He just needed to figure out how best to manage the task.

~~~

Four hours later with his chores at the cottage completed, John reminded his mother he promised to help with the horses at the Stuart stables and hurried out to his car. He did not mention Sandra had promised to do so also nor that they weren't due to assist until early afternoon. He swung by the Duncan cottage and picked up Sandra and drove up into the mountains near the grassy bald which marked the highest point on the Stuart property. John parked his car, and he and Sandra hiked the last half-mile to one of their favorite picnic spots in the high meadow. There, they could sit and talk for hours with no one to interrupt them.

"We have to tell them, John, and soon." Sandra's grip on John's hand tightened as she spoke. "I can't keep hiding how nauseous I feel from my mother much longer. I barely kept anything down at breakfast."

He leaned his head against hers. "I know. I wish we could keep the news all to ourselves. We should be able to enjoy the idea of becoming parents. We should be able to tell our friends we're getting married. I hate that we can't do anything without consent. At least I'll turn eighteen in four months. That doesn't help with you, though."

"No, my mother will have to give her approval for us to marry. I can't see any way around that. We need to decide who to tell when and how, and we must do it soon, John. Especially my mother." Sandra put her free hand to her stomach as another wave of nausea hit. When it passed, she continued, "I can't hide it from her much longer."

"How do you think she'll react? I mean, she won't be happy, but if she knows we want to get married, do you think she'll accept it once she gets over the shock? I can quit school and work if my mother and grandmother won't agree to support us long enough for me to finish." They were questions John and Sandra asked one another repeatedly over the last two days.

"Do you think they won't? I mean, I know they'll be upset like my mother, but I'd hate for you not to be able to finish high school. It would be bad enough for you not to get to go to college. I don't think I could stand it if I was responsible for that."

John pulled his hand free of hers and put both arms around her, pulling her close. "Sandra, we're equally responsible. We made the baby together, and we'll get through this together no matter what. I'm least worried about Gramma Kate. She'll be disappointed in me, but I don't think she'd kick us out. I'm not sure about my mother, but if Gramma will support me long enough to finish high school, I can find a job."

Sandra sat quietly considering their situation as John continued to sort through options once he finished school. Neither spoke of Sandra finishing; both knew she wouldn't be allowed to attend once her pregnancy became known. They weren't even sure John would be allowed to finish once they married.

"John, why don't we try to get them together and tell them all at once? At least, our mothers and your grandmother. I don't know if having Winston there would be better or worse."

When he remained silent for several seconds, Sandra pulled back and looked up at his face. To her surprise, he was grinning widely.

He realized she was staring and hugged her close again. "Sunday dinner. I'll ask Gramma to invite Mom and Winston and your family to Sunday dinner. We might as well get it over with on all fronts at once. Your brother is going camping with friends this weekend, so we won't need to worry about him finding out with the rest. Your mother can decide when and how to tell him. Claudine won't be in the way either because she's to visit her mother and grandparents this weekend."

At the thought of the four adults staring at them across the dinner table in shock, Sandra began to balk at her own suggestion. "We'll be badly outnumbered. Are you sure that's a good idea? Maybe we should tell just our mothers or maybe my mother and your grandmother?"

"I think all at once would be best. Just get it over with. If it's OK with you, I will even the sides a little though."

It took her only a second to catch up. "Matt."

Matt Hunter, John's second cousin and best friend, had lived on the Stuart estate since his widowed father had been transferred several hundred miles away more than a year earlier. Kathryn Stuart insisted her great-nephew be allowed to remain in Elkford to finish high school, and Earl Hunter agreed.

"Yep, if we tell him as soon as he gets back from visiting his dad Saturday, he'll be prepared to jump in to support us at Sunday dinner. Heck, he'll be my best man, and supporting the groom is part of the best man's duties." He laughed for the first time in days.

Chapter 2

"Sandra, breakfast is almost ready." Millie Duncan opened the bacon and sliced several pieces in half. "I don't want to start the bacon until you're here. Hurry up, honey." She slid her knife under one piece and dropped it into the frying pan.

Fifteen-year-old Greg Duncan wandered from the kitchen to the hall where his backpack and sleeping bag awaited, inspected both, and returned to glower at his sister's empty place at the table. "They'll be here in fifteen minutes, Mom. Can't you make Sandra some when she gets up? I need to eat now."

"Fine, pour your juice and start filling your plate. I'll cook these two pieces for you and make more when she's ready." Millie lit the burner and set the screen over the frying pan to control the grease splatter. "Hey, just two biscuits for you, young man. Sandra and I get one apiece."

Greg dropped the third back onto the platter with the last one and took his seat at the table. "Ow," he exclaimed when he tried to split one of the hot biscuits by hand. He picked up his knife, slit both open, and slathered on a generous helping of butter and raspberry jam. His eggs and grits were half inhaled by the time Millie dropped his bacon onto his plate. "Thanks, Mom."

"You're welcome, dear. Try not to choke on it eating so fast. They'll wait for you to finish and brush your teeth. You're sure you have everything you need for camping?"

In between bites, Greg said, "Yes, Mom, I'm sure. Mr. Casper gave me and Caleb and Asa a list of things to take plus we've been camping with scouts, so we know the essentials we need. We'll be fine. Don't worry." He picked up the warm bacon and shoved half of it into his mouth.

"I know, Greg, but you're my baby. It's my job to worry about you." A horn sounded, and Greg bolted up. "No, sir, you finish those last few bites. I'll let them know you need five more minutes." A stern look stopped any argument, and Greg shoved in the rest of the bacon.

Seven minutes later, the pickup carrying Greg, Asa, and Caleb disappeared up the road. Millie stopped waving after them and started back toward the kitchen. When she remembered she had yet to see Sandra, she turned and walked down the hall to the room her middle child now had to herself. Cindy, the eldest of the three Duncan children, married Calvin Vickers the previous summer and moved out of the cottage Mrs. Stuart had supplied to the Duncans since Millie began working for her in July 1948.

"Sandra, are you up? It isn't like you not to rise with the sun." A noise from her daughter's room startled Millie, and she pushed open the door and hurried inside. Sandra knelt on the floor, her head over the trashcan. "Honey, what's wrong?" Millie rushed forward and knelt beside the girl. "Do you think you ate something bad?" She pushed Sandra's blond locks back with one hand just as another round of retching hit. She laid her other hand against the child's forehead to check for fever.

When she could speak again, a teary Sandra shook her head. "No," she whispered, "it's nothing I ate, and it isn't some virus I caught. I'm sorry, Mother. I'm so sorry."

Millie pulled the child into a tight embrace while trying to process the girl's meaning. She had looked a little pale recently, and her appetite had been below normal two or three times during that period. "Oh no. Please tell me you and John haven't gone too far." Even as she pleaded for some assurance, she already knew the answer. "Does John know?"

"Yes." Sandra spoke so softly her mother could barely understand her. She wiped at her mouth with the sleeve of her nightgown before continuing. "I realized it Monday and told him the next day." She pushed up and raised her eyes to meet Millie's. "We want to get married. We planned to tell everyone Sunday, well, you and Mrs. Stuart and the Hathaways. John convinced his grandmother to invite everyone to dinner so we could break it to both families all at once."

Millie forced herself to think rationally and not react with pure emotion. "Well, I suppose marriage would be the best option, but I don't expect John's mother will be eager to agree to it. We'll need to get you to a doctor soon to verify..." She stopped and blew out a breath, patting Sandra's hand. "Sit here a minute while I get a washcloth for you." After a quick trip to the cottage's bathroom, Millie knelt by her daughter again and began to wipe her face and hands.

Sandra leaned back against her bed. "We don't think Mrs. Hathaway will agree to our marriage without argument either, but John believes his grandmother might be more easily persuaded."

Millie rose and picked up the soiled trashcan. "I expect she might accept the idea better than Jeanette, but John will require permission from his mother to marry before he turns eighteen. I'm not sure even Mrs. Stuart will prove capable of bringing enough pressure to bear on her to achieve that goal." She hurried to the bathroom and dumped the trashcan contents into the commode before setting it into the tub to clean later.

When she returned to Sandra, the girl's head was against her knees, and she was sobbing quietly. Millie sat down beside her daughter and pulled her close. "Hush, dear, crying won't fix anything. Regardless of Jeanette's objections, John turns eighteen in December. As unfortunate as this is, I believe he loves you, and I expect Mrs. Stuart will support your marriage. She isn't one to approve of shirking responsibilities. She's also fond of you, and I know she believes you and John make a good match despite our lack of financial and social status. She had neither to match Alistair Stuart's when she married him, so she understands that there are more important things. Ultimately, it is her support which will be required, not Jeanette's. All will be well, dear."

"I hope so, Mother." Sandra sniffled and wiped at her eyes. "I do love him. People will say I just want his money and position, but I don't care about those things. Neither does he."

"I know, Sandra, but you are right about people talking. You need to be prepared to ignore the gossip and slander." Millie rubbed her eyes, trying to focus her mind on the practical issues at hand. "I believe we need to modify your plan to make an announcement at dinner tomorrow. At the least, I can't be party to springing such a surprise on Mrs. Stuart, both because her support is most critical as well as the fact she is my employer. She needs to know today." She hugged Sandra once again. "If you feel well enough, go get cleaned up. I'll get you something light to eat. That will help settle your stomach. I'll consider how to tell Mrs. Stuart."

"Yes, Mother. I feel better already." Sandra sat up, allowing Millie to stand. The girl slowly slid up until she could sit on the side of her bed.

"Stay there a moment until you're sure." Millie watched for any sign of further nausea. "Sandra, does anyone else know yet?"

Sandra shook her head. "No, but John plans to tell Matt when he gets back today. We thought he would make a good ally."

Millie chuckled. "Yes, I imagine he will." Matt Hunter was known for keeping one or two steps ahead of most everyone. He annoyed some of his teachers by out-arguing them regularly. One day, he would be a master tactician. Not a bad ally for John and Sandra considering how close he was to both. Only Kathryn Stuart would be more valuable. Perhaps Matt should be present when the elderly woman learned she was to become a great-grandmother in the new year.

~~~

"I don't see why you should be the one to drive to Woodbury to collect that boy. He can wait for the bus into Elkford," Jeanette complained. "I had thought you and Claudine could spend the day enjoying the pleasant weather. School will begin in just over a week. This is your last year of high school, your last summer before you begin a new chapter in your life. You should not be forced to spend it ferrying a poor relation."

John kept his eyes fixed on his dresser mirror, ignoring his stepsister's face peeking over his mother's shoulder. Despite the fact he and Sandra had been dating for more than two years, both his mother and Claudine persisted in the delusion he held any interest in anyone but Sandra. Satisfied with his hair, John dropped his comb onto the dresser and turned to face his mother at last.

"I offered to pick up Matt. Nobody made me. He shouldn't need to wait for hours to catch the bus into Elkford since it only runs twice on Saturday. Besides, Gramma Kate wants me to get a couple of things for her while I'm in Woodbury. And Matt is not some poor relation. He might not be as wealthy as Gramma Kate, but neither are we. His father has a good job, it just took him away from here, and Gramma Kate wanted Matt to stay so he could finish high school in Elkford with all his friends, including me." He checked his watch. "I need to go if I'm to pick up those things and not be late meeting his train."

Finally allowing eye contact with Claudine, he added, "I have a date with Sandra tonight, so I won't be back until late. I might even stay over at Gramma Kate's to have more time to catch up with Matt. He's been away at his dad's for two whole weeks." The angry look Claudine gave him at the mention of Sandra strengthened his resolve. Why hadn't the arrogant girl gone to visit her mother in Woodbury this weekend as planned? He didn't want to think too much about the answer to that question. "Actually, let's plan on me sleeping at Gramma Kate's. I'll see you for dinner tomorrow at her house." He slipped between the two women staking out his bedroom and made his escape.

~~~

Two hours later, John stood on the platform in the Woodbury depot waiting as passengers filed off the train. When Matt stepped out of his coach, strolling behind an elderly couple and swinging his suitcase as if he hadn't a care, John breathed a sigh of relief. He needed the rational thinking and easygoing personality of his cousin. The drive from Woodbury back to Chestnut Cove would give them plenty of time to talk. When Matt reached his cousin, the two embraced a moment before heading to John's car.

After questions about Matt's trip and events during the intervening weeks at Chestnut Cove and in Elkford had been exhausted, the perceptive Matt said, "You've told me about everything except one important person: Sandra. Is something wrong? You two haven't had a disagreement or anything, have you? Did you do something to upset her?"

John kept his eyes fixed on the road ahead. "No, nothing like that." They were approaching a small settlement between Woodbury and Elkford, and he pointed to a café at the crossroad. "Let's stop to grab lunch first. Then I'll tell you."

"All right." The car pulled into the parking lot. "Why don't we see if we can get a couple of sandwiches to go? That fishing spot we tried out last month is near here. We could stop there to eat where it's quiet. As bad as the fishing proved to be that day, surely nobody will be anywhere around it this afternoon."

Nodding in agreement, John climbed from the car and followed Matt inside. Fifteen minutes later, they sat on a rock overlooking a burbling stream, no one else in sight.

When their silence dragged on for several minutes, punctuated only by their soft chewing and the crinkle of paper, Matt said, "OK, John, spill it. You're worrying me. Tell me what's wrong."

John looked across the stream toward the mountains beyond. Somewhere up there, Sandra waited for him to return and finish planning their announcement set for the next day. "I'm going to be a father, probably in March."

Matt stopped just before taking another bite, his sandwich left suspended inches from his mouth. After a moment, he managed to swallow. "Wow. No wonder you've been so distracted. How's Sandra feeling?"

"Pretty lousy at times. I don't know what to do to help her either. Well, with the sick part. We're going to get married, but we can't yet, and I don't think my mother will agree to let me marry before I turn eighteen. We don't know about Mrs. Duncan."

"Does anybody else know yet? Aunt Kate?"

John finally looked at Matt. "No, we plan to tell everyone tomorrow at Sunday dinner. I suggested Gramma invite Mother and Winston and the Duncans to dinner, and she agreed. She'll probably be mad when she finds out why." He shuddered when another realization struck him. "Oh, and Claudine will be there, too. She cancelled plans to visit her mother this weekend at the last minute."

Matt closed his eyes and shook his head. "Don't worry about Claudine. I'll help deal with her. As for Aunt Kate, she might be irritated for a short time about you manipulating her into the dinner, but she'll understand your motivation was noble. She won't stay mad at you."

John nodded. "I know, and she's really the one who counts. I know that, too. I hope she'll accept Sandra. She likes her."

Setting aside the remains of his lunch, Matt put a hand on John's shoulder. "I think she'll be happy to have Sandra as your wife, though maybe not quite so soon. And congratulations, both on the baby and on your engagement. Have you bought her a ring yet?" Leave it to Matt to skip over the nerve-wracking details.

"No, I haven't even thought of that. I need to. It looks more official if there's an engagement ring, doesn't it?"

With a laugh, Matt said, "I think carrying your baby makes it more official than anything, but yes, a ring would be good, too. Maybe Aunt Kate will give you something, some sort of heirloom. I bet Sandra would like that."

John smiled at the thought. "Yes, she would." Forcing his attention to another frivolous detail, John added, "Whenever we manage to get married, I want you to be my best man."

"I'd love to stand up with you," Matt said with a grin. "I can't wait. Now tell me your plan for this big announcement tomorrow."

~~~

When the boys walked through the kitchen entrance of the Stuart home, the family's cook and housekeeper barely acknowledged the return of Matt after a two-week absence before directing John to go to the study. "Your grandmother wants to see you immediately," Lila informed him. "Alone," she prompted when Matt started to follow his cousin.

"Aw, Lila, Aunt Kate will want to see me. I haven't graced her with my presence for two weeks." He put one arm around her and leaned over to check out the various vegetables spread across her cutting surface. "What's for dinner?"

"Never you mind, child. Take your bag upstairs while John sees his grandmother. If you can't find something useful to do after that, come back here and I'll put you to work peeling potatoes." She pointed to a pile of spuds on the counter.

"Uh, I need to unpack and hang up my clothes. I washed most everything at Dad's, so there isn't much in my suitcase for you to deal with. You're welcome," he added, flashing his widest grin before kissing her cheek.

"Uh huh, I'll check on them later to see if they pass inspection. If not, I'll give you lessons on the proper way to clean clothes. Now get out of my kitchen before I put you to work."

"Yes, Lila," Matt said before he slipped through the door into the dining room and escaped to follow his cousin. John had just stopped at the closed door of the study and tapped on it when Matt spotted him. "Any idea what she wants?" he whispered.

They could hear the muffled sound of the elderly woman speaking to someone, though they couldn't distinguish her words. John shook his head. "No, I can't imagine.

Maybe it's one of those days she wants to tell me more about one of the businesses or the estate management. If so, I'll remind her you're back and get her to let you sit in if you want. You have a better head for some of that than I do. I sure hope you'll decide to stay here and work with me on all this one day when I have to take over."

"I appreciate that, and I promise to think about it. First, we have high school to finish and then college. I hope Aunt Kate has years to go running things before you have to take over."

"So do I, Matt. So do I."

"Come in," Kathryn McDougal Stuart's voice sounded from the study.

"I'll be upstairs unpacking. Call if you need support." Matt hurried around the corner toward the stairs as John opened the study door and stepped inside.

"Come in and close the door, John," his grandmother directed. "Sit, please." She pointed at one of the leather chairs in front of the oak desk.

Ignoring her directive for a moment, he skirted the end of the desk and leaned down to kiss her cheek. "Good afternoon, Gramma Kate. I hope you're well today. I just brought Matt home. He's upstairs unpacking."

"Good afternoon, dear." She pressed a hand to his cheek before resuming her business-like composure. When John took the indicated seat, she began. "I would like to speak with you a moment before we are joined by other guests. I received a telephone call this morning requesting an audience with the two of us. Our guests should arrive shortly."

John raised his eyebrows at her vagueness. "Who are these guests, Gramma? Do I know them?"

"Indeed, we both know them well, which is why the request for a formal audience baffles me. I hope you may shed light on the matter since your inclusion was requested. Do you not know of this meeting already?"

"No, Gramma, I have no idea what this is about. Who requested it? Who is coming here?"

Kathryn's eyes bored into her grandson's. "Mrs. Duncan and Sandra. Have you and Sandra suffered some sort of falling out? Is there some issue between the two of you of which I am unaware?"

John's complexion paled, and he swallowed hard. There could only be one subject about which Millie Duncan was bringing Sandra to see him and his grandmother. Their plans for an announcement at dinner tomorrow would be for naught.

When John spoke, his voice came out raspy. "I expect I know, Gramma." He forced himself to meet and hold her gaze, his fingers gripping the arms of his chair. "We had planned to tell everyone tomorrow at dinner."

Kathryn sat unflinching as she awaited the unraveling of the mystery. "But now Millie and Sandra plan to do so earlier? Am I to learn this secret before they arrive?" She glanced at the shelf clock above John's head. "In less than a quarter hour."

John straightened in his chair and announced in a stronger voice, "Sandra and I intend to marry as soon as possible. She's carrying my child."

His grandmother held his gaze for almost a minute without speaking. When she broke her silence, she said, "I see. Your plan entailed announcing this fact to both families tomorrow at dinner? I cannot agree that such a tactic was well thought out.

Does no one know other than you and Sandra and now myself and presumably her mother?"

With a shrug, John said, "I told Matt on the way home from Woodbury."

"Mmm, that does not surprise me. I should have expected you to confide in him as soon as possible." She settled back into her chair as she processed the information. "Your mother will be displeased, to say the least. She has no inkling she is soon to become a grandmother?"

John shook his head. "No, and displeased is an understatement. Just this morning she tried to get me to take Claudine for an outing. I don't think she will accept my marrying Sandra. That means we can't marry until I turn eighteen in December. If Mrs. Duncan won't agree, we'll be forced to wait until February."

"No, I cannot foresee your mother providing any support and encouragement. You need to accept that now if you have not already. I must say I am disappointed in you also, though what is done is done. We must deal with the consequences. Blessedly it is Sandra, not Claudine or some other young lady." She locked her intense gaze on his eyes. "I want your assurance there has been no other girl, John."

His tanned skin could not hide the redness which raced up his neck and enveloped his face all the way to the tips of his ears. "No, ma'am. I've never even kissed another girl. I love Sandra. I intended to propose after we graduated. We just need to marry sooner than I hoped."

"Indeed, much sooner. You understand this will cause something of a scandal. We cannot hope to hide her pregnancy. I will do what I can to bring pressure to bear on your mother to consent to a prompt wedding, assuming Millie is prepared to do so for Sandra. However, I do not believe Jeanette will be swayed. She has her head set on certain expectations for your bride, and Sandra does not meet them."

"I know, but she's wrong, Gramma. Sandra makes me happy, and we understand one another and get along well and want the same things in life. Besides, we love each other." The doorbell sounded as an echo to his pronouncement.

"Good. You must stick to your resolve. It will be difficult going for the two of you. Jeanette's friends will talk, and their children will talk. You know my opinion of such people, but it will be necessary to interact with them in the course of living your life. Be prepared."

With a nod, John rose. "Yes, ma'am, I am, and I'll support Sandra every way I can." A tap on the study door signaled that Lila or Matt had admitted Millie and Sandra to the house. "Oh, before I let them in, Matt reminded me I need to get Sandra a ring. I have a little money saved, but I need to borrow some to have enough to buy something nice...unless you have a Stuart or McDougal heirloom you might want her to have. I'll pay you back as soon as possible working extra on the estate."

Kathryn smiled at last. "I believe there is something suitable I would be willing to give you for her to wear. Why don't we discuss that after we settle some details with Millie and Sandra? Perhaps you could present her with a ring tomorrow at dinner."

John's shoulders relaxed at her agreement. "I think she'd like that, Gramma. Thank you, both for the ring and your support." He hurried to the door and opened it. Millie and a pale Sandra stood waiting. After a quick glance at Millie, John pulled Sandra into his arms. "I love you. Everything will work out."

Millie looked past the couple to her employer, still seated behind her desk, and Kathryn beckoned her secretary inside. "Please take a seat, Millie. I have just completed a conversation with John which I believe sheds light on the reason for your visit." The efficiency and clinical detachment Kathryn showed in her business dealings worked well to encourage the others to set aside the emotional aspect of the issue and focus on the practical matters needing resolution.

"Yes, ma'am. I'm pleased John has informed you himself. I dreaded breaking the news to you." She settled herself into her usual spot for taking dictation and otherwise assisting her employer.

John escorted Sandra into the study and seated her to the left of her mother in the chair he had just vacated. He brought another from the far side of the room and placed it to Sandra's left, sat, and took her hand in his.

No sooner had John settled himself than his grandmother turned her attention to the spiral stairs in the corner which led to the library above. "You may as well join us, Matt. You'll hear better if you're in the study with the rest of us instead of eavesdropping from up there. You might even contribute a useful idea."

Never one to require a second invitation, Matt could be heard scrambling to his feet on the library floor before he tromped down the wrought-iron steps into the study. He grabbed another chair and placed it beside John before circling the desk to kiss his great-aunt's cheek. "It's good to be back, Aunt Kate." Next, he hurried around behind the others to lean down and hug first Millie and then Sandra from behind. "Congratulations, cousin-to-be." His greetings complete, he took his place next to John. "All right, Aunt Kate, you may begin."

"Scamp," Kathryn muttered. Returning her attention to the others, she addressed the girl first. "Sandra, I want you to know I am pleased you are to become John's wife. I could not have chosen someone more suitable. I see no need to discuss the unfortunate timing. As I told John, what is done is done." Kathryn looked to Millie to ensure concurrence from the girl's mother, who nodded in agreement. "Therefore, I believe we should simply address ourselves to how best to proceed.

"Since the two of you have already expressed interest in marrying as soon as possible, we should begin to plan for that event. I will apply whatever pressure I may to Jeanette, but I fear we must expect resistance from that quarter we may not overcome. Therefore, a wedding may not take place until John's birthday in December. Millie, are you prepared to give permission for Sandra to wed at that time?"

"Yes, Mrs. Stuart, December or earlier if Mrs. Hathaway agrees." Millie held her steno pad, ready to note items requiring action by the group.

Matt picked up the desk calendar and flipped over to December. "John's birthday will be on the second Saturday. School will break for Christmas a week later, and Christmas Eve falls on Saturday of the following week."

John looked at Sandra. "Assuming my mother won't see reason, we could get married on my birthday or the next Saturday–the day after school lets out for Christmas–or sometime the week after that. Do you have a preference, or do you need to think about it?"

Sandra chewed on her lower lip as she considered their choices. "You might have a lot of schoolwork right before the holidays, so your birthday might not be a good choice." Her voice gained strength as she continued. "If we choose the day after you get out for Christmas break, we might feel too rushed. I believe I would like to have as close to a proper wedding as possible, though I don't want anything but a small ceremony. What if we took the first week of the break to finish final preparations and married on Friday?" She glanced from John to Mrs. Stuart to Millie. "Do you believe the minister would be available and willing to marry us then? I wouldn't ask for Saturday since it will be Christmas Eve."

It was Kathryn Stuart who pronounced the verdict. "I am quite sure the minister will be available the day prior to Christmas Eve. He certainly will not be out of town with so much to do at church."

A half-smile crept onto Sandra's face, the first real sign of happiness from her since she entered the study. "If you're sure, Mrs. Stuart." Turning back to John, she asked, "Would that suit you?"

He squeezed her hand. "Yes, it's a good plan. I like the idea of taking a little time to enjoy the final preparations for the wedding. Of course, if my mother can be convinced to agree to us marrying immediately, I'd prefer that option. Should we also consider earlier dates? If Mother agrees, the sooner we can marry, the better."

"For the moment, John," his grandmother said, "we will limit ourselves to what we assume will be her decision. I suggest we leave the two of you to discuss what you desire in the way of a wedding. We can pick up here in a few days. Once you are confident you are satisfied with that date, I will approach the minister. In the meantime, I believe we should continue onto another topic. From Sandra's reference a moment ago, I gather the two of you already understand the impact this will have on her attendance at Elkford High School."

Sandra and John nodded. "Yes, Gramma, we're aware they won't let Sandra stay once they discover she's with child."

"No, they will not. It may require a pointed conversation with your principal to ensure they allow even you to finish once you and Sandra marry. I shall deal with that once we sort out her situation." Turning to Millie, she continued, "I suggest that we employ a tutor to finish her education so she may receive her diploma. I will bear the expense." She held up her hand when Millie opened her mouth to protest. "She is to become my granddaughter-in-law and wife to my heir. I can and will see to her education. There shall be no discussion on the matter. Millie, you and I shall identify and interview suitable candidates and select one acceptable to us both. The tutor will attend her here for her lessons. I will set aside use of the parlor as a classroom. She may utilize the library for her studies as she has done in the past along with John and Matt. Does that meet with everyone's approval?"

"Yes, ma'am," Sandra said. "Thank you, Mrs. Stuart."

"Dear, for all intents, you are to become my granddaughter soon. You must begin to address me less formally than as Mrs. Stuart. Remember, soon you will become Mrs. Stuart, also."

At the reminder, Sandra glowed. "Yes, ma'am. Would it be all right if I called you Grandmother Kathryn?"

The elder Mrs. Stuart's eyes crinkled as her lips pulled back into a rare smile. "That will do nicely, dear." She took a deep breath before shifting once more into a business-like demeanor. "Now, we need to consider the matter of when and how to inform Mrs. Hathaway." All parties present knew the matriarch's mindset when she referred to John's mother by her married name. "I believe she should be informed prior to dinner tomorrow. However, I see no need to do so until she arrives here after church. If it is acceptable to you, John, I suggest you and I inform her in the study as soon as she arrives. Matt, you shall entertain Mr. Hathaway during that time."

Matt pasted on a smile. "And Claudine? John said she abandoned her plan to visit her mother this weekend, so I presume she will come to dinner, too."

Kathryn closed her eyes a moment while she digested that detail. "Yes, you will need to keep both occupied. Millie, I suggest you and Sandra delay your arrival until the last moment to give us time to manage the Hathaways."

"Yes, ma'am. Would it be best for us to abandon plans to attend dinner tomorrow?" Millie stole a look at Sandra.

"I see no reason to do so. The initial confrontation with Mrs. Hathaway must occur at some point. Here in my house in my presence, I will be able to exert any pressure required to control her outburst." Kathryn reached for the desk calendar Matt still held. "John, I suggest you choose to remain here tonight and tomorrow night at the least. Perhaps longer until the situation settles."

John agreed immediately. "I already told Mother I planned to stay here tonight since it's Matt's first night back. We need to catch up. I'll stay here at least tomorrow night, too." All knew the scene Sunday evening at the Hathaway household would be tense when Jeanette escaped Kathryn Stuart's presence to fully vent her fury.

"Good." Kathryn stood, and the others followed suit. "I suggest we adjourn to the veranda and hold a quiet celebration. You should inform Lila of your news. I have every confidence she will keep your secret until we are prepared for the wider world to learn of it."

Sandra circumvented the massive desk to hug Kathryn. "Thank you, Grandmother Kathryn, for everything. I would like to tell Mary and Jonah, too, if they are around. Would it be acceptable to include them in our celebration on the veranda?" Mary, Lila's nineteen-year-old daughter, and her boyfriend, Jonah, worked on the estate and had long been friends with John, Matt, and Sandra.

"Of course, dear. Lila will know where they are. If they are nearby, send Matt to find them and bring them to the house." She took the girl's hand and led her out of the study, the rest of the group trailing behind.

Chapter 3

Sunday, August 21, 1955

A summons, not an invitation. Jeanette understood that well. She forced herself to maintain her composure and trailed her former mother-in-law into the study of the Chestnut Cove mansion. John followed the women and pulled the door closed.

"Please be seated, Mrs. Hathaway." Again, a directive, not an offer of hospitality. Jeanette's jaw clenched, but she followed Kathryn Stuart's command and perched on one of the chairs in front of the desk. The older woman walked around behind it, seating herself on the throne which had served as the seat of power in the family since Alistair completed the mansion decades earlier.

"I hope I've done nothing to offend you, Mrs. Stuart." Jeanette thought a vague, preemptive suggestion of an apology for whatever had the old dragon riled might prevent a prolonged discourse of any offenses.

Kathryn's face gave away nothing. She sat perfectly still, her eyes focused on the younger woman. "No, the matter about which I desire to speak with you today concerns John."

The boy had remained standing, choosing to position himself away from his mother and paternal grandmother. When his name was mentioned, he shifted his weight from one foot to another, trying not to look like a five-year-old caught with his hand in the cookie jar.

Jeanette's mind raced on its own wild tangent as usual. John would begin his senior year in high school soon. Perhaps his grandmother would finally settle at least a small portion of his future inheritance on him. Her thoughts leapt forward to conjure things he might buy for her. After a few seconds, she realized Kathryn continued speaking, but in an entirely different direction.

"When I learned of a certain situation involving John and Sandra, I cannot say I was pleased." Kathryn's words left Jeanette baffled. "However, they have made the responsible decision, and I fully support them. I expect you to do the same." Kathryn paused before pronouncing what sounded like a judge handing down the death penalty to Jeanette. "Sandra is with child. She and John wish to marry at once. However, as you may be aware, one must be of age–eighteen in this state–to wed without parental consent. Mrs. Duncan is in agreement with their intentions and will provide consent for Sandra. You must do so for John."

"What?" Jeanette's jaw hung slack while she digested the words. "No, that is not possible." Her head snapped around toward John, who remained silent but nodded in confirmation of his grandmother's words. She shot out of her chair as her head whipped back around to face the dragon. "I shall *never* consent to such a travesty! My son is meant for better fare than that tart. Send her off somewhere to have the child. Good riddance to her. Come, John, we are leaving this vile place immediately." She stormed across the room, one hand waving wildly toward her son.

When he finally spoke, John's words matched his grandmother's in tone. "No, Mother, I'm staying here. Do not ever speak disparagingly about Sandra again. I will marry her regardless of your consent even if it means we must wait until my birthday."

A shocked Jeanette stopped halfway to the study door, her mind reeling at John's defiance.

Her former mother-in-law spoke in a low monotone those who had ever crossed the grand dame knew well. "John shall remain or go as he wishes. As for you, leave this house if you like, but remember upon whom you depend to maintain the roof over your own head. If you persist on your current course, you shall depart my cottage with all your personal belongings by the end of the day."

Jeanette balled her hands into fists, her nails digging gouges into her palms. The shock announcement incensed her. That Sandra would claim to have been impregnated by her son infuriated her. That John and the old dragon intended for him to marry the little tramp exceeded all reason. However, the threat to remove the Hathaways from the cottage they occupied for the last four years was all too real. The humiliation would be more than Jeanette could bear.

"As usual, Mrs. Stuart, you will surely have your way, but I will never be a party to this sham. If John persists in this absurd inclination to marry that deceitful, manipulative..." Jeanette stopped, realizing she might still go too far, John's warning echoing in her mind. "I will not consent to a marriage. I cannot stop John from doing as he pleases once he reaches eighteen, but I can delay the matter until December in hopes he will see through this charade and come to his senses in the interim."

"I expected no better from you, Mrs. Hathaway." Kathryn stood from behind the desk and took John's arm. "We shall formally announce the engagement at the conclusion of dinner. The marriage will occur in December unless you see sense before that time. If you prefer to inform your husband in private beforehand, you may do so now. We have a few minutes before Lila summons us to the dining room. Mrs. Duncan and Sandra should arrive momentarily."

Jeanette, her back to Kathryn and John, understood she had been dismissed. She stalked forward and jerked open the study door. Instead of joining the others on the veranda, she stormed into the parlor where she hoped she would be left alone while she composed herself. It appeared Winston and Claudine would be the only people unaware of the impending announcement. As far as Jeanette was concerned, they could hear of it at dinner. Perhaps seeing the shock to poor Claudine would give John pause to reconsider his intentions.

~~~

As soon as John appeared on the veranda, Claudine began a sultry stroll in his direction. However, the ringing of the doorbell caused him to hurry back into the house, leaving her, Matt, Winston, and now Kathryn as a silent foursome. Moving to his great aunt's side, Matt held a brief, whispered conversation with her before following John's route. He veered off to update Lila and Mary on the latest development and inform them Kathryn was ready for dinner to be served. Lila and Mary began moving serving dishes from the kitchen to the dining room, and Matt picked up the platter holding the leg of lamb and placed it where Lila directed.

Returning to the veranda, Matt nodded to Kathryn to indicate Lila had dinner laid on the table before greeting Millie and Sandra. Jeanette remained absent from the gathering, and Matt disappeared back into the house, taking it upon himself to inform her dinner was ready so John would not need to abandon his fiancée.

Never one to stand on ceremony when he could avoid it nor pass up an opportunity to annoy John's difficult mother, Matt barged into the parlor. "Dinner is served. Aunt Kate prefers everyone be seated before we begin. I'm sure you remember that from your time living here." His lip twitched with the effort to refrain from grinning at her discomfort. He had tried for years to accept her for John's sake, but the constant conflict and wild expectations she exhibited wore on even his easygoing personality.

Now he followed his great aunt's lead and dismissed her out of hand or, when neither John nor Kathryn were near, needled the annoying woman mercilessly. "If you choose to skip dinner, I'm sure she will understand, but she needs to be informed. Shall I do so for you? Of course, that will mean you'll miss the official announcement of John and Sandra's engagement. Did he show you the ring he's to present to her? Aunt Kate gave him the one Uncle Alistair gave her for their twenty-fifth anniversary. Very understated elegance, which suits Sandra perfectly. She isn't one for ostentatious display the way some girls are, all show and no substance like many of the country club set."

Jeanette glared at the impudent teen. "No, I shall attend her dinner if only for another chance to share my objection to this travesty. I fully intend to convince John to abandon the tramp before this union can come to fruition. I don't even believe the girl is with child, and if she is, who knows who the father might be." She gave Matt a pointed look.

The cheerful smile left his face, and he took three strides across the parlor to stand before her. He leaned close, his voice menacing. "Never say such a thing again. Sandra loves John, and he loves her. If you ever loved anyone, including either of your husbands, maybe you could grasp that concept. If you do anything to harm her or John, you will not only have Aunt Kate's wrath to suffer. You will have me to deal with, and I lack Aunt Kate's restraint. Now follow me into the dining room and act like you accept Sandra and their baby into the family, even if you don't like the idea." He spun and walked out, his normal smile back in place.

~~~

Dinner passed with small bursts of stilted conversation. Kathryn and Matt did most of the speaking with John chiming in off and on when he could tear his attention from Sandra for more than a few seconds. The boys flanked the matriarch, who sat at the head of her table. Sandra was seated to John's left with her mother on her other side. Claudine had taken the seat she expected would place her next to John, only for the boys to swap their usual spots to ensure Sandra could sit by him. The presence of the detested Matt Hunter to her left kept Claudine focused on her plate when she accepted that she could not draw John's attention from Sandra. Winston chose the seat to his daughter's right, leaving Jeanette somewhat isolated at the far end of the group next to her husband. No one was unhappy with that part of the arrangement.

Before Lila and Mary brought in the dessert course, Kathryn cleared her throat to draw the attention of the room. "Before we continue, my grandson has an announcement to make." She tipped her head in his direction. "John?"

Forcing his butterflies away as he stood, John slipped his hand into his pocket and fingered the ring hidden there. "Last week, Sandra and I had a long talk about things and came to a decision." He turned to her and produced the gold filigree ring with a half-carat diamond set within. "Sandra and I are engaged." Holding out the ring for her to see, he continued, "Grandmother offered this to become your engagement ring if you like it. Grandfather gave it to her for their twenty-fifth anniversary, and she would like to pass it on to her future granddaughter-in-law."

Any promise Sandra made to herself to maintain her composure during dinner fled when John slipped the ring onto her finger. He pulled a handkerchief from his pocket and wiped at her tears.

During the touching scene, Matt heard a snort of disgust from down the table. He stole a look at Mary, who stood against the opposite wall waiting to help serve dessert. She conveniently held an excellent view of Jeanette's face. He could tell from Mary's expression that she heard and saw Jeanette's reaction. The two friends would compare notes later. Along with Mary's boyfriend, Jonah, they would do all they could to ensure no one, especially the Hathaways, caused any more distress and interference than necessary to John and Sandra's happiness.

Satisfied Mary maintained a close watch on Jeanette, Matt turned his attention to Claudine. Her jaw was set, and he wondered that he couldn't hear the gnashing of her teeth. He feared for the life of the starched, white napkin in her lap. She held it with both hands, twisting it into a rope she no doubt would like to use to strangle Sandra.

Matt leaned close to Claudine's ear and whispered, "Aren't you going to offer your congratulations? I know exactly how much you think of John. You should be pleased he is marrying the woman he loves instead of some money-grubbing parasite who only sees dollar signs and the status of the Stuart name."

She turned her eyes toward him but could think of no response. Both knew his barb had found its mark.

~~~

Their hostess rose from her seat after dessert, signaling the time had come to move the celebration to the great room. Winston managed to take two steps before his wife seized his arm. "Winston, I have a terrible headache. I simply must return home to rest for the afternoon." Claudine didn't need further direction. Her nose firmly upturned, she marched across the polished floor and up the steps to the front door. She stopped, waiting for someone to follow and open it for her. Winston cast a rueful look at the Stuart liquor cabinet before he allowed his wife to drag him after Claudine.

Matt practically bounded up the steps after them, arriving just in time to smirk at Claudine. He opened the door and bowed to the departing guests. "I hope the three of you have a pleasant evening. I'm sure I'll see a great deal of you in the coming weeks as the wedding plans progress."

Jeanette issued what Matt could only describe as a snarl. She marched out the door, leaving Winston and Claudine to follow.

As soon as Winston started the car, Jeanette spewed out, "The girl claims to be with child. John's child, of course. We know it cannot possibly be true. Oh, she may well be in the family way, but certainly not by my son. However, the dragon not only believes the girl, but she fully supports this horrid marriage fiasco. Would you believe she asked me to consent to an immediate marriage? Let me tell you, I flatly refused. I will fight them every step of the way. The very idea of my son, the Stuart heir, marrying a common tart like that. He should marry someone from a proper family. Someone with style, money, polish, connections." She turned around to where Claudine sat behind Winston. "Someone like you, dear, is imminently more suited to be John's wife than such a girl. No, I will not allow it."

Claudine took her cue and began to sniffle. "How could that girl destroy my future? I love John. We're meant to be together. Just think of what a handsome couple we make. I should be the one on his arm when the governor comes to Elkford to tour some factory John runs. No, a bank. He could buy the bank Daddy works at and merge it with the one Grandfather owns in Woodbury. He would be one of the wealthiest people in the state. He could run for office himself. I'd make a beautiful first lady of the state. Then he could go to Washington as a senator. We'd get to go to balls at the White House." She gasped. "He could be President!" She leaned forward, her chin on the back of the front seat. "I could be like Eleanor Roosevelt, except young and beautiful like Grace Kelly, and go all over the country representing him. Even to Europe. I'd meet kings and queens. Gosh, I read in a magazine Grace Kelly is dating the Prince of Monaco! If she marries him, she'll be a princess, and I'd host her at the White House!" Remembering John's engagement, Claudine's gleeful imaginings morphed in an instant. "That horrible girl! How dare she steal John from me. Daddy, don't let him marry her," she wailed.

Winston's knuckles whitened as he gripped the wheel tighter. "I don't have any control over what John does. That's up to Jeanette."

Her stepmother reached back to pat the girl's hand. "I intend to make John see reason, dear." After the brief interlude to comfort her preferred choice of daughter-in-law, Jeanette's anger returned in full. "I should go back up there and drag John out of that house. He's my son. I have every right to decide what's best for him."

"Where do you intend to sleep tonight, Jeanette?" While Winston hadn't been present for the earlier threat, he knew it existed, whether spoken or not. "Shall the four of us spend tonight at the Mountain View Motel with the little money we have in our checking account? We could possibly manage two or three nights if we pack what food is in the house to eat along with the rest of our belongings we can fit in the cars. I hope the old woman will allow us a couple of days to find someone to move our furniture to some empty lot in Elkford since that's all we'll be able to afford."

As much as she might want, Jeanette couldn't refute his implication. If she even tried to implement her threat, the dragon would surely execute her own. They would be evicted before dusk. If she couldn't provide a roof over her son's head, she would have no chance in court when, not if, the dragon challenged her custody of him. It would all be for naught. John would return to his grandmother's home and the clutches of that manipulative hussy. She banged her fist on the dash and squalled at the pain.

His screeching wife and wailing daughter drove Winston to satiate his earlier desire for a drink as soon as they reached home. He took a glass and a bottle of whiskey outside. The noises emanating from the house continued until long after dark, though Winston's snoring and the chirp of crickets drowned out much of it as he slumped in his favorite chair on the porch.

Chapter 4

Tuesday, August 23, 1955

John remained at his grandmother's until Monday evening. She encouraged him to spend another night at her house, but he needed to see his mother and judge her state of mind now that she had time to fully digest the facts and accept his determination to marry Sandra as soon as possible.

The evening at the Hathaway cottage went as poorly as Kathryn feared, with John hounded by both his mother and Claudine. His arrival Monday evening renewed their fury, and only with his threat to return to his grandmother's house did they allow him to seek haven in his bedroom for the night. He left shortly after first light Tuesday morning to meet Jonah and Matt to repair fences, a task sure to keep him from home most of the day.

Deprived of one target, Claudine decided to confront the other. Midafternoon, she borrowed Jeanette's car for a short drive to clear her head. Instead, she drove to the Duncan's cottage. Millie had left to attend her employer before nine o'clock, assured Sandra's new breakfast menu seemed to have lessened her morning sickness. Greg, informed of the situation on Monday when he returned from camping, had accepted the news stoically. He liked John, and the idea of gaining a big brother sooner than expected appealed to him. Cindy's marriage to Calvin had given him one as well, but Cal's tenure in the army meant they left Elkford soon after their wedding.

John would be around until June. After that, he and Sandra would only be as far away as Coughton Tech and would visit Elkford and Chestnut Cove frequently during John's time at college. Matt would be almost like another brother, and he, John, and Jonah often included their young friend when they went fishing.

Greg had been instructed to remain close to home, tending to his weekly chores in case Sandra needed something while his mother was at work. Thus, when Jeanette's car pulled into the Duncan driveway, he was in the backyard tending his mother's tomato plants. He heard a car door slam but ignored it to finish tying up a vine determined to go rogue. Engrossed in his battle, he jumped when he heard shouting. He dropped his twine and knife and raced around to the front of the house.

The surreal sight of Claudine Hathaway gripping his sister's arm with one hand, index finger of her other waving in petite Sandra's face as she tried to push the taller girl away, shocked Greg. Shouts of "whore" and other words Greg didn't know rang through the surrounding mountains. The wiry youth charged forward and launched himself between the two girls, ripping Claudine's hand from Sandra's arm in the process.

Claudine stumbled back, and Greg pushed his sister through the open front door. "Stay inside. I'll get rid of her." He slammed the door and turned to face Claudine. "I wasn't raised to hit a girl, but I'll make an exception unless you leave now. Don't you ever come near my sister again." When the enraged girl didn't move, Greg stalked forward, fists raised.

Claudine fled to the car and fired the engine. Instead of backing out of the driveway, she turned and cut across the lawn, carving ruts in it and running through a hedge of rhododendrons.

Satisfied the girl wouldn't return and ram the house with the car, Greg ran inside. He found Sandra sobbing and holding her stomach. "Are you hurt? Is the baby hurt?"

With a shake of her head, Sandra choked out, "No, she just startled me. I can't believe she came over here and threatened me and accused me of entrapping John. I'm not surprised she feels that way, but John can't stand her. Even if he didn't love me, he would never date her, much less marry her. Besides, she's his stepsister. I don't think it's even legal for them to marry."

"It sounds creepy even if it is." He reached out to touch her forearm. "You have some red marks where she held onto you. I'll get some ice to put on it. Then we better call Mother and Mrs. Stuart. Claudine's gone for now, but who knows if she'll come back." He hurried into the kitchen, grabbed a dishtowel, and opened the refrigerator to grab some ice from the freezer compartment.

Once Sandra had the pack on her arm, he returned to his earlier thought. "We need to let Mother and Mrs. Stuart know what happened. I don't think she'll come back, but we can't be sure. You don't need to put up with that. Mrs. Stuart will put a stop to it. John needs to know, too."

Sandra looked at her watch. "Mother will probably be home soon. Let's wait until she gets here. John is with Matt and Jonah working on fence today. He won't get back to his grandmother's house until late. They're trying to finish while John and Matt are available to help."

"He'll want to know, Sandra. That girl's crazy. She could have hurt you or the baby."

"I don't think she'd have gone that far. She's just upset." She set the ice pack aside and touched her arm.

"I can tell how far she went by the outline of her fingers." He walked to the hall where their telephone rested on a small table. "I'm calling them."

~~~

"Is she hurt?" Millie bolted out of her chair as she spoke, attracting her employer's undivided focus. "I'll be right there. Lock the doors in case she comes back."

As soon as Millie dropped the phone's receiver into its cradle, Kathryn spoke. "What happened? Is Sandra injured?"

"Claudine paid a visit. She had grabbed Sandra's arm and was screaming at her about trapping John into marriage when Greg reached them. He managed to separate them and get Sandra inside and then scare Claudine off. There are red marks on

Sandra's forearm where that girl gripped it so hard. Claudine drove through the rhododendrons as she left. I'm afraid she's completely out of control." Out of professional habit, she added, "I'd like to go check on my children if I may be excused for the rest of the day."

Kathryn had already risen from her chair. "Of course, dear. Go ahead. I'll be along shortly. First I shall do what I may to prevent a recurrence." She followed Millie out the study door. "Lila?" she called. "Would you locate one of my drivers and have them move my car to the front door?"

Lila's footsteps sounded through the house as she rushed from the kitchen toward her employer. "Yes, Mrs. Stuart, of course. Mary is in town doing the shopping. I'll call down to the stables."

"If no one is available, I will drive myself. Miss Hathaway has approached Sandra at home and abused her and frightened Greg. I shall go to the Hathaway's cottage and then to Millie's to ensure myself of Sandra's wellbeing. First, I must place a telephone call."

"Yes, ma'am. I'll try to have someone here right away." The ladies returned to their separate domains, Millie having already raced out the front door to go home.

Kathryn flipped through her address book to find the phone number of the small bank where Winston worked. She dialed and waited impatiently for an answer. "Yes, you may," she replied when someone answered at last. "This is Kathryn Stuart. I must speak to your president, Mr. Mobley, immediately." When the voice on the other end began to explain about a meeting in progress, Kathryn cut him off. "Either you shall interrupt him long enough to speak to me or I shall remove all my funds from his institution promptly at ten o'clock tomorrow morning."

Seven minutes later, Kathryn emerged from her front door to find Gus, one of her employees, backing her Lincoln out of the carriage house. They arrived at the Hathaway cottage in another nine minutes. "Block Mrs. Hathaway's car in the driveway, Gus. Do not allow anyone to leave. Mr. Hathaway should be here soon to take his daughter away. I do not expect any resistance from him. However, Miss Hathaway and Mrs. Hathaway may protest. We may require your assistance in encouraging the girl to do as she is told. I shall not have her confronting my grandson's future bride again."

"Yes, ma'am, Mrs. Stuart," Gus replied. "We'll all make sure Miss Sandra stays safe."

Kathryn nodded her thanks and stepped out of the car. She started toward the front steps but stopped when she noticed a discoloration on the front fender of Jeanette's Packard. She walked closer to determine its cause. The dark paint showed scrapes where something sharp had raked across it. Bending down, she felt under the wheel well and found bits of rhododendron leaves plastered to the metal. She motioned for her driver to attend her. By the time he reached her side, she had rounded the car to the front. More signs of minor damage showed on the bumper and bumper guard on the right side.

"What do you take from the damage to Mrs. Hathaway's car, Gus?"

He stooped down to study the indicated area. "Appears somebody drove it right through a hedge, Mrs. Stuart. Scraped paint and chrome all along the front right of the car."

"That was my thought also, Gus. Thank you. That confirms what Greg told Millie, as I expected."

He kicked at the tire with his foot. "Got a cut on the sidewall. Might have run over a sharp stake or broken branch when it went through the hedge. Didn't puncture the inner tube, but it could be dangerous to drive like this. Shall I offer to change it for Mrs. Hathaway?"

"Perhaps it would be best if you remove the wheel so no one can drive it in an unsafe condition. Can you do so utilizing the jack and wrench from my car? Once Mr. Hathaway arrives and we assess the situation, he may provide you with the key to access the spare so you may complete the task. Ensuring this car isn't available for that girl's use until she can be properly dealt with is our most essential task."

"Yes, ma'am. She won't drive it as long as I'm here."

"Thank you, Gus. I can always count on you and the rest of my staff to do what is right."

Leaving him to his task, Kathryn strode onto the front porch and pressed the doorbell. The silence of the house had surprised her. Neither Jeanette nor Claudine bothered to curb their temper nor the volume of their opinions in most settings. Only within the walls of Chestnut Cove or near their benefactor would either remember to whom they were beholden for this home and Winston's job and temper their ranting about whatever displeased them.

When she pressed the bell again, Jeanette's voice screeched, "I'm coming, I'm coming." Soon, footsteps sounded in the living room and the door shot open. A slew of emotions passed across the woman's face, but she refrained from speaking at first. Finally, she said, "Good afternoon, Mrs. Stuart. To what do I owe the pleasure of your surprise visit?"

"I doubt it is such a surprise. Where is your stepdaughter? Are you aware of her actions within the last hour?"

The hesitation before pasting on a blank look assured Kathryn that her former daughter-in-law knew something. "Her actions? Why, I have no idea what you mean. She took a drive earlier and came home to rest before dinner. I believe she might be on the telephone with one of her friends."

Kathryn pointed to Jeanette's Packard. "Have you seen your car since she returned? The girl ran through Millie's rhododendrons with it after assaulting Sandra. Gus is removing a damaged tire before you or anyone else drives it in an unsafe condition."

"What? Who made such horrible accusations against poor Claudine?" Jeanette shouted. "Why would you believe your secretary or her tramp daughter without seeking the truth from someone more trustworthy? Claudine simply went for a drive. She went nowhere near the Duncan house. How dare you accuse her of such a thing!"

"Then how did your car receive damage? It still has green rhododendron leaves pasted inside the wheel wells. Are you responsible for the scratched paint on the fender?" Kathryn stepped back to give Jeanette a clear view of Gus jacking the front right of her car off the ground.

Jeanette stomped across the porch and down the steps toward her car. When she spotted the scarred paint on her fender, she stepped back in horror. When she had time to formulate a quick lie, she spun toward Gus. "You did this! You hit my car with those tools. Claudine is a very careful driver. She would never damage it."

Gus remained silent and impassive, content to let his employer handle the squalling harridan, while he spun the wrench to remove the first lug nut. Before either woman could further their skirmish, two more contestants entered the field. First, Claudine emerged from the front door. Seconds later, her father's car pulled to a stop in front of the house.

"What is she saying about me?" Claudine stabbed at the air with an index finger. "I didn't do anything. That tramp attacked me when I stopped to talk to her. Then her brother tried to knock me on the ground. I had to jump back in your car and lock the doors. He...they banged on the car with limbs trying to get to me. It was terrifying!" She rushed to Winston, sobbing. "Daddy, they tried to kill me! Look where they hit the car with those sticks!"

Winston pushed the girl away and walked over to view the front right of his wife's car. Satisfied, he continued toward Gus and the damaged tire. Gus pointed to a fresh slice in the sidewall.

"I'll put the spare on if you'll give me the trunk key, Mr. Hathaway," Gus said. "You need to get this one replaced."

Winston passed his keyring to the mechanic. "Put the keys in my car when you're done. I'll be leaving again in a few minutes." He motioned to his daughter. "Get your things, Claudine. You're going back to your mother's. We're leaving in five minutes."

While the girl began to argue and wail, Jeanette understood. Either Claudine left the Stuart estate immediately, likely never to return, or Winston and Jeanette would be evicted before the day was out. No doubt Winston's job as a loan officer at the bank, gained with the help of Kathryn Stuart and her money, would end also.

All three Hathaways disappeared inside their Stuart-owned cottage. Gus opened the trunk of Jeanette's car and quickly installed the spare and placed the damaged tire in the trunk. Kathryn walked back to her Lincoln and sat waiting for Winston and Claudine to depart Stuart property.

When father and daughter appeared again, Claudine was voicing her hatred for Elkford and her sole desire in life of returning to the civilized society of Woodbury. Even as they pulled away, she continued to berate her father for insisting she live with him the last two years.

When Gus guided the Stuart car out of the Hathaway driveway, Jeanette stood on her porch glaring at her landlord. Kathryn ignored the woman. "All right, Gus, let's get to Millie's and check on Sandra and Greg."

"Yes, ma'am, Mrs. Stuart."

~~~

Gus stopped behind Millie's car less than ten minutes later. Greg was working to salvage what he could of the rhododendron hedge at the front of the yard. The boy stopped to wave the elderly lady inside. "The door's open, Mrs. Stuart. Mom and Sandra are in there."

"Are you all right, Greg? I gather you acquitted yourself well today. We've seen Mrs. Hathaway's car. It's a wonder Claudine didn't try to hit you or Sandra with it or even the house."

He set his clippers on the ground and walked closer. "She's just a bully, Mrs. Stuart. She's taller than Sandra, and Sandra wasn't feeling too good anyway, but Claudine didn't want to challenge me when I got around here. I told her I wasn't raised to hit a girl, and I wasn't. Mom would be horrified if I ever did, but I'd have made an exception if she hadn't left. You can still see the welts on Sandra's arm where Claudine grabbed her."

"You are an excellent brother, Greg. I'm sure your mother would have understood if you needed to defend your sister. We've just left the Hathaway house. Mr. Hathaway has taken his daughter to her mother's home, and she is to remain there. You should not need to deal with her again."

"That's good. Thank you, Mrs. Stuart. Sandra will feel much safer knowing Claudine isn't anywhere close." He looked back at the hedge. "I need to get back to work. I hope some of them can be saved, but I'm not sure."

"Be all right if I help him a little while you're inside, Mrs. Stuart?" Gus asked.

"Of course, Gus. I imagine I'll be some time with Millie and Sandra."

Gus picked up a shovel Greg had nearby and began to fill the ruts in the lawn, and Kathryn walked to the front door and let herself in. She heard voices and followed them toward the kitchen. "Millie?"

"Yes, Mrs. Stuart. We're in the kitchen." Millie's head appeared around the corner. "I was just preparing a new ice pack for Sandra's arm."

"Does she require a doctor? I will call and ensure they wait for us."

"No, ma'am, it's better. I'm just trying to reduce the redness and prevent any bruising if I can."

Kathryn followed her into the kitchen and went straight to Sandra. To the girl's surprise, the elderly lady hugged her a moment before stepping back to a more proper distance. "I must apologize, dear. I should have foreseen a reaction of some kind from that girl. However, I've sent her away. Mr. Hathaway has taken her back to her mother, and I've forbidden her presence on any of my property. That should end any similar attacks for the immediate future." Her focus moved to Millie. "I am concerned she might find some means of causing further mischief in the later. It will be your decision, Millie, but I suggest...offer my house to keep Sandra in a safer environment. She will need to move out of your cottage once she and John wed. I believe it would be prudent if we moved her into my home much sooner. Whatever trouble Claudine Hathaway or anyone else might seek to cause, I cannot foresee anyone attempting any maliciousness there. They know too well the consequences. Those would be the same here or anywhere else, but I believe that fact might not be fully understood by some people. If Sandra were resident in the main house, she would be safer. So would you and Greg since Sandra would be their target."

Millie's eyes misted, and she whispered, "I think you're correct, ma'am, but Sandra needs a say in that decision."

"Of course." Kathryn returned her attention to the girl. "If you decided you wanted to return here, you could do so at any time. I only want what is best for you, as does your mother. Why don't I have Mary prepare a room for you so you can use it whenever you desire? You could at least come with your mother each day and have a place to rest when you need to or spend the night when you wish."

Sandra moved the ice-filled towel from her arm so she could see the red marks. Her hand shook so much she dropped the towel. Millie grabbed it before it could reach the floor, though several pieces of ice spilled out.

"You're sure Claudine is gone, at least for tonight?" Sandra's voice came out as almost a whisper.

"Yes, her father took her away. He will ensure she reaches Woodbury tonight. He also understands the penalty he will suffer if he fails to do so. He will not allow her to dissuade him from his task."

"I'd like to spend one last night here with Mother and Greg, but I would feel safer at your house. I think Mother and Greg would be safer, too." Looking directly at Kathryn, Sandra added, "I'm afraid Claudine might not be the only one to try something foolish."

A quick exchange of looks between Kathryn and Millie ensured that they felt the same way. "All right, dear. I'll look forward to seeing you tomorrow. We'll have your room ready. I thought the one on the second floor near the library, if that suits you. Not too many stairs and easier for anyone downstairs to hear you call should you become ill."

"That would be fine, Mrs. Stuart." At a stern look from the matron, Sandra corrected herself. "I mean, Grandmother Kathryn. Thank you." She stood and hugged the elderly widow.

~~~

Two hours later, only John, Matt, and Jonah remained ignorant of the afternoon's events. As soon as she returned to her mansion, Kathryn summoned Lila and Mary to the study and informed them of the pending move. Mary hurried upstairs to prepare the room selected for Sandra's use while Lila went back to the kitchen to continue preparation for dinner.

When a weary John and Matt arrived after a long day of hard labor, Kathryn called them into the study to inform them about all they missed.

"This afternoon, Claudine confronted Sandra at the Duncan cottage. Sandra is unhurt but rattled. The situation–John, hear me out," Kathryn called. She knew it was a futile effort. John could already be heard tearing up the steps to the foyer. "It's been dealt with, Matt."

"Yes, ma'am." Matt leaned toward the study door, tight as an overwound spring.

"Go on before he can leave without you. Don't let him speed too much, Matt," she called as he sprinted out of the room.

Matt chased John out the front door and jumped into the passenger seat of the car just before it roared to life. "John, she's OK. Aunt Kate's handled it. Don't wreck before we get there. You'll upset Sandra more than she is already."

John eased off the accelerator, but not by much. "What was that insane girl thinking? I wonder how much she's already slandered Sandra to her friends."

"We'll deal with it, John. That part was bound to happen eventually. You can't hope to hide Sandra's pregnancy or prevent anyone with an idea of how long one lasts realizing she got pregnant before you married, especially if your mother sticks to her refusal not to give you her consent to marry before your birthday."

John slowed the car further as he calmed a little more. "I know you're right, Matt, but I can't stand anyone saying anything bad about her."

"I know, and she knows, too, but she's the one who will suffer the most attacks. It isn't fair, but that's the way it is. She'll need you to stay calm. If you get upset and try to punch anyone who says anything about her, it will make things worse. People will do it to get a response from you. Ignore them as best you can."

Matt's rational thought process and calm demeanor helped settle his cousin. "It won't be easy, Matt, but I'll try."

Some of John's anger returned when they reached the Duncan house. The rhododendron hedge which lined part of the front yard had a car-sized gap, though some of the lawn damage was less obvious thanks to the work Gus and Greg put in.

Before they reached the front door, the boy opened it to admit the latest guests. "I'll let Sandra know you're here. She's in the back with Mom packing."

"Packing? Is she going somewhere?" John stepped around Greg, unwilling to wait for him to tell Sandra her fiancé awaited her.

Matt grabbed John's arm to stop him long enough to clear up the mystery. "She's coming to stay with us, isn't she?"

Greg looked confused. "Yes, didn't Mrs. Stuart tell you? She thought it would be safer in case Claudine escaped from her mother or some other crazy girl tried the same thing."

When he felt John's muscles relax, Matt released him. "John didn't give Aunt Kate much chance to tell us anything. He bolted for the door the instant she got as far as your run-in with Claudine. She told me she had handled things, but I couldn't wait to learn how without John taking off without me."

The sound of the commotion had reached Sandra's bedroom, and the girl rushed past her brother to throw her arms around John.

"Are you hurt?" he demanded.

"No, she just frightened me. I've never seen anyone so angry. I don't know what she'd have done if Greg hadn't been here to intervene." She snuggled into him, not caring that they had an audience.

"You're moving in with us tomorrow? What about tonight? What if she comes back?"

Shaking his head, Matt muttered, "I doubt Aunt Kate missed that step. We should have waited a couple of minutes to hear the rest of the story."

From the hall door, Millie concurred. "No, she didn't miss anything. She summoned Winston home from the bank. I suspect there was a threat implied if not spoken. He hurried to his house and left with Claudine within a few minutes. He took her to Woodbury to stay. Mrs. Stuart banned her from the entirety of Chestnut Cove and all other Stuart property. We're sure it will be safe here for Sandra tonight. We're packing some of her things now and will bring her to the main house tomorrow. I'll pack the rest and bring them later."

Matt took the time to study Sandra's face and arms. He could see no sign of any injury Claudine caused. While no one had defined just what the confrontation entailed, he suspected it had been physical. If John spotted any kind of mark on his fiancée, it would take a mammoth effort to prevent him driving to Woodbury tonight to hold his own confrontation with the witch.

After John and Sandra had time to console one another and she assured him she was well, Matt and Millie managed to pry John out the door. Sandra needed to complete her packing and spend a little time alone with her mother and brother on her last night in what had been her home for seven years.

Matt beat John to the car and slid behind the wheel. "I think I need to drive us home."

"Fine, but go by my mother's house first. I want to talk to her."

"Nope." Matt shifted into reverse and backed out of the driveway. "From what Millie said Aunt Kate got out of your mother, it doesn't sound like she really knew what Claudine did, certainly not in advance. She just loaned her the car."

"Maybe, but I want to find out myself. We won't be there long." Away from Sandra for barely a minute, John's anger began to bubble to the surface again.

The car reached the turn which would lead them to either the Hathaway's cottage a short distance outside the mountain cove or the main house within. Matt downshifted to second and took the direction toward his great aunt's home. "No, not tonight, John. Things are tense enough between you and your mother. You don't want to add to that. As long as there is any chance she might change her mind and agree to you and Sandra marrying before you turn eighteen, try not to antagonize her. I know that's easy for me to say, especially after what Claudine did, but at least wait for a day or two." Matt stole a look at his cousin. Though still angry, John appeared to have accepted the validity of Matt's perspective. For both, it would prove to be a long night with one still pondering a late-night confrontation and the other intent on preventing one.

Chapter 5

When her mother's car cleared the trees to bring the house into view, Sandra saw John and Matt sitting on the front steps. In unison, they rose and walked to meet the car as it stopped in Millie's accustomed place. John opened Sandra's door, took the small valise from her, and gripped her icy hand with his free one. Matt retrieved her large suitcase from the backseat and followed Millie and his friends up the steps.

Alerted to their arrival by Mary, who had stood watch inside, Kathryn Stuart met her new houseguest in the foyer and greeted the girl with a hug. "Welcome to Chestnut Cove, dear. Your room is ready for you, and Mary will assist in getting you settled. Lila will have a light lunch ready for us at one o'clock as usual."

In a barely audible voice, Sandra replied, "Thank you, Mrs. Stuart. I'm afraid I might not be up to eating much, but I'll do my best."

Kathryn exchanged a look with Millie. Ignoring the events of the previous afternoon, she said, "I understand, dear. After all, though it has been many years on, I still recall feeling unwell early in my time carrying John's father and uncle. Your mother, Lila, and I being familiar with such things, we will maintain a supply of suitable fare for those times you are feeling poorly. And remember, you are to address me as Grandmother Kathryn." Turning her attention to the boys, she pointed up the staircase. "Take her bags up to her room. You know which one is to be hers. Then return to the study. I have some tasks for you boys today. Mary will assist Sandra with her unpacking. You may visit with her at lunch."

"Yes, Gramma," John said. Matt followed his cousin up the stairs, Mary right behind them.

Alone in the foyer with Sandra and Millie, Kathryn took Sandra's hand. "This is to be your home now. I want you to understand you are free to treat it as such. You are long since familiar with much of it, so you don't need a tour. Once you are settled and rested, come downstairs to the kitchen and ask Lila to show you where everything is. Though she prepares most of our meals, you may wish for something when she is unavailable. You are welcome to anything there, and we will keep a supply of things like soda crackers you may need to settle your stomach for the next few weeks. If you wish for anything we don't currently keep on hand, let Lila know so she can add it to her shopping list."

Eyes downcast, Sandra whispered, "Yes, ma'am. Thank you, Mrs. Stuart–I mean Grandmother Kathryn."

"All right, go up and settle in, child. We'll see you later when you feel like joining us."

When Kathryn released the girl's hand, Sandra turned to her mother. "You'll be here all day?" Tears welled in her eyes.

"Yes, darling," Millie embraced her daughter. "I'll be here all day as usual, and if you need me tonight, call me and I'll come back over here."

Sandra, head pressed into her mother's shoulder, managed a nod. "I will. Thank you, Mother, for your support. I know I've disappointed you terribly."

"It will all work out, Sandra. You and John have a good basis for your life together, even if it's starting earlier than I would have wished."

Sandra composed herself and released her mother. "I'm sorry to be such a crybaby. I appreciate all the support we've received from both of you." A sound behind her alerted her that the boys had returned and stood just above them on the steps. She looked up at John with a watery smile. "Yours, too."

"Hey, what about me?" Matt interjected. As usual, he managed to elicit a laugh from the group.

"Even you, Matt," Sandra said. She started up the steps and hugged him as they passed before John pulled her into his arms and kissed her. When they separated, she whispered to him, "Especially you." She slipped around him and hurried up the stairs.

When she reached her second-floor bedroom, Mary had the large suitcase open. A pile of hangers lay on the bed as the young maid hung a pair of slacks in the closet. "Mary, I didn't mean for you to do my unpacking. I can manage." The two girls had known one another ever since Sandra's mother came to work for Mrs. Stuart and were already good friends.

"I know, but it's my job to help you as a guest of Mrs. Stuart as well as my friend who isn't feeling well. How are you this morning? Nauseous again?"

"A little, but not as much now as earlier." Sandra picked up a dress and began to arrange it on a hanger. "My nerves this morning don't help either."

Mary produced a tin of crackers from atop the dresser. "Brought these up earlier so they would be handy when you need them." She took Sandra's hand and led her to one of two stuffed chairs in front of the window. Once Sandra seated herself, Mary sat in the other chair and each girl took a cracker from the pack. "Your nerves should settle down soon. You're used to visiting the house, and you and your family have dined here often. This is just one more step, and it isn't like you weren't destined to move here eventually. We all knew you and John were meant to be together, and this is his family home. It will be yours and his one day."

"I hope I'll feel more comfortable in it soon. You're right about my familiarity with the house but living here feels different. I know it's for the best, but it will take getting used to living somewhere other than with my mother." She closed her eyes as a slight wave of nausea struck. When it passed, she added, "I'm glad the guest rooms all have their own baths. I'd be so embarrassed to run down the hall trying not to lose my breakfast before I could get to one. It's enough worry that I could get nauseous when I'm somewhere other than in my room."

Mary giggled at the prospect. "Well, my mother says that should pass in a few weeks."

"I hope so. It's enough getting used to the idea of John seeing me in the morning before I get my hair and makeup done. I can't imagine how he'd look at me if I lost my breakfast in front of him."

"Sandra, he's besotted with you. He's so in love with you nothing will affect how he looks at you. Don't worry. Besides, soon you'll be married to him, and after that you'll have a precious little baby to worry about. All this will be behind you by then."

At the thought of holding her new baby, Sandra's face took on a soft smile. "I can't wait. All the turmoil will be worth it when John and I are married and I'm holding our little boy or girl."

~~~

"I am your mother. I decide where you live and who you may spend time with and when you may leave my house." Jeanette's screeching rattled the rafters of the cottage. However, her son continued to ignore her as he tossed another stack of shirts into his suitcase. He had reached his own decision during the previous night; he would never sleep another night in the Hathaway cottage. He slipped away a couple of hours after Sandra arrived at his grandmother's house to inform his mother of his decision and collect the remainder of his summer and part of his winter clothing.

While Jeanette denied any knowledge or involvement in Claudine's confrontation with Sandra, John remained unconvinced. Not one to show good sense, the woman had ignored his edict and shifted the conversation's focus to Sandra and her unsuitability for John, even as he began to pack clothing into his suitcase. Each cruel word cemented his resolve to implement his plan.

Jeanette reached for his half-full bag, but the look of anger in his eyes surpassed any she had seen before. She backed away a step but resumed her rant. "Really, John, she's just a passing fancy. You must realize how much better you can do than the daughter of a secretary and a deceased military man."

Turning slowly to face his mother, John's voice came out in a rumble. "In case you've forgotten, I'm also the son of a deceased military man. It's something Sandra and I have in common. She was very supportive of me after Dad's death, and we're both proud of our fathers' service to the country."

"Well, yes, technically, but your father wasn't career military. He only served during the war because he felt it was his duty."

"Yes, it was, and it was Lee Duncan's duty, too. He died doing his job, and Dad was wounded and captured doing his. It just took Dad until five years after the war to die from his injuries. Like I said, it's one of the many things Sandra and I have in common." He snatched up a collection of underwear from a drawer and dropped the pile into his suitcase. "At least Sandra's mother supports herself and her children along with the death benefits she receives from Sergeant Duncan's sacrifice. You merely sponge off Gramma Kate." Jeanette had the good graces to flinch at the truth.

John continued his outburst, unwilling to give his mother an opportunity to deny facts. "Winston, too, partly. She's provided this house for you ever since you and Winston married, so whether I stay here or with her, I'm living in a place she owns, not you. I'd take very seriously her threat to kick you and Winston out of here." He picked up a framed photograph of his father in uniform and tucked it safely between the layers of clothes. Then he slammed the suitcase lid and snapped the latches into place. "I'll return for the rest of my things later. Right now, I need some air." Snatching his bag off the bed, he marched out of his room and down the hall to the kitchen door.

Jeanette remained rooted in place until she heard the roar of an engine. She knew better than to chase after her son and try further to make him see reason. For now, she needed to form a new plan. He was right about one thing; the old bat would toss them off the Stuart estate without hesitation given the least incentive. She had as much as said so.

"Winston, where are you?" Jeanette called. Another complication caused by the little tramp's attempt to coerce John into marrying her was Claudine's anguish. Winston's daughter remained among Jeanette's choices for a future bride for John, the previous day's unfortunate episode notwithstanding. While Winston's family had lost its fortune, the girl's maternal grandparents still owned a bank in Woodbury as well as a nice estate there. Surely, they would overlook the little matter of Winston abandoning Hortense to pursue Jeanette. Hortense was such a pathetic little thing. Her only attraction for Winston had been her family's money. A match between the Stuart heir and the granddaughter of the owner of Woodbury-West Bank should be sufficient to overcome any past issues. If not, she had other options at the Elkford Country Club from which to select a bride for her son.

"Winston," she called again. "Where is that man?" Her husband had returned in the early hours of the morning after delivering Claudine to her mother. He had declared himself too exhausted to work after his long night and settled himself where Jeanette finally found him, sitting on the porch with a snifter in hand and a formerly full bottle tucked under his chair. He didn't stir or acknowledge her presence in any way, though she failed to notice. "Really, Winston, it is early to be drinking hard liquor." She rubbed her temple with one hand. "John and I had words and he left again. He took some of the clothes he keeps here. He intends to stay with the old dragon and that little tramp. They've moved her into the main house."

Gathering her second wind, she paraded across the porch. "I cannot fathom what that woman is thinking. How could she support a union with someone so beneath her only grandson? And she intends to have the girl live under her roof and just down the hall from John's bedroom!" Jeanette stopped to take a couple of deep breaths before she continued her tirade. "I expect the girl will attempt to sneak into his room every night. She probably has experience in such things. There is simply no telling who the father of her child is, assuming she hasn't invented the whole thing as a ruse to trap my poor boy."

Nodding to herself, she continued, "I must insist on a doctor from Woodbury verifying she is even with child. It would not surprise me if she made up the whole thing. Sally told me about a doctor over there her daughter saw when she needed someone outside Elkford. I must call her to find out his name. We could insist the tramp undergo an independent examination before this gets out of hand." She leaned down and kissed Winston's cheek. "Thank you for your support, dear. I'll go call Sally." As she disappeared inside, Winston tipped his glass back to get the last precious drops to trickle into his mouth.

~~~

John stalked the length of his grandmother's veranda again, Matt watching each step from his seat in the swing at the far end. "I can't believe some of the things she said, Matt. It's like she doesn't even want to give Sandra a chance. She's determined to think poorly of her. Even after yesterday's attack on Sandra, she still holds some delusion about me and Claudine."

"She'll get used to the idea of you and Sandra marrying, John. It's still a shock to her." Matt hated to lie to his best friend, but he couldn't admit he didn't think Jeanette would ever accept Sandra. She would never see how Sandra was perfect for John. She filled a place in his life no one else could. Matt envied him that and looked forward to the day he could find someone to do the same for himself.

"I know, but she doesn't need to say such mean things about Sandra. I wouldn't be surprised if she encouraged Claudine to confront Sandra yesterday." A noise behind them caused both boys to turn.

Sandra stood in the doorway. "Mary said you left earlier and returned with a suitcase full of clothes from your mother's house. She's never going to give in, is she?"

John didn't answer at first, but her steady gaze held his until he had to shake his head. "No, it doesn't look like it. I brought more of my clothes from their cottage. I won't go back there except to get the rest of my things." He stood a little straighter at the pronouncement.

"John, I don't want to cause you to break with your mother." Her lip trembled, and John rushed to her and pulled her close. "I won't be responsible for injuring your family."

Matt joined them and encircled both with his arms. "You've done nothing to cause this, Sandra, and you're a part of this family now. Just ask Aunt Kate. Jeanette is the only one creating tension, well, and Claudine, but she's gone back to Woodbury. Hopefully she'll stay there. Aunt Kate says you're in this family, and I say you're in, so you're in. The little one, too. Never mind Jeanette or Claudine or anyone else. Right, John?"

"Right," John agreed, squeezing Sandra tighter.

Chapter 6

"What do you want to do tonight?"

Sandra studied her toast. She didn't mean to make John wait for her reply, but she didn't really know what to say. She had yet to venture out of Chestnut Cove since their engagement became official. The thought of coming face to face with their friends or Claudine's didn't appeal to her. It would happen eventually, but she had dealt with too much upheaval over the last two weeks.

"What about just going for a drive? I'm afraid to go out to eat yet. I'm not sure what will upset my stomach. It's been better the last few days with Mother and Lila and your grandmother setting a bland menu. I'm afraid if we went out to eat even somewhere in Woodbury where we weren't likely to run into somebody we know, I'd run the risk of a repeat of the fish odor making me nauseous. If we went out in Elkford where we're sure to meet people we know, it would make me so nervous I'd throw up for sure."

Matt returned to the dining room to join the conversation. He and John had eaten their normal hearty breakfast earlier. Since Sandra's move to the main house, Lila had prepared the boys' breakfasts well before Sandra came down each morning to prevent any chance of those odors upsetting her stomach. She would even air the kitchen afterward to minimize the more potent smells. The expectant mother would stick to toast smeared with a thin sheen of butter and a cup of tea for now.

"Why don't I call Maria and ask her to join us for a drive? She's one of your best friends. You haven't spoken to anyone outside the family in two weeks." Matt grinned at her. "You two did intend for your little drive to include me, right? We can make it a foursome if Maria is free. You'll have to face people sooner or later. Wouldn't it be good to start in a controlled situation with someone you know well and who will be sympathetic and supportive?"

Sandra's hand trembled, and she dropped the toast back onto its plate. "You don't know if she'll be supportive."

Matt pulled out a chair next to her and took her hand. "Yes, I do. I saw her a couple of days ago in Elkford."

"She already knew?" Sandra whispered.

John, seated on her other side, put an arm around her but remained silent. He knew

Matt well enough to know this wasn't a sudden, thoughtless idea tossed out on a whim.

"Yes, she knows. At least, she'd heard a version of the story. She knew not to believe some of the details. I wanted to tell you sooner, but I knew it would lead to other questions. Maria would really like to see you, and she intended to talk to some of your other friends and correct some misinformation."

Sandra drew a shuddering breath. "You mean Claudine's information. Even from Woodbury, she's spread the news and embellished the truth with plenty of lies." She began to cry, and John pulled her close.

When she could speak again, Sandra said, "Thank you, Matt. When you talk to Maria, tell her I appreciate her believing you and not Claudine. You should call her and see if she wants to go out tonight, but I'd rather stay here. Maybe next weekend I'll be ready. Right now, all I can think about is seeing that doctor in Woodbury on Monday and Mother and Grandmother Kathryn interviewing potential tutors for me during the week. I can't face anything else yet."

Matt squeezed her fingers. "It will wait a week. I'll call her though and tell her you appreciate her support." Releasing her hand, he said, "You need to finish your toast and tea before both get cold. Since it's raining this morning and there's nothing we need to do inside to help, I think I'll get my guitar and play. We could hold a sing-along in the great room if it won't bother Aunt Kate. Hey, we can practice lullabies and children's songs! We'll need to know those before long."

The thought of Matt serenading his godchild in a few months elicited a laugh from the expectant mother. "That's a good idea. I looked through the sheet music Mrs. Stu—Grandmother Kathryn has yesterday. There were some songs suitable for children included. Do either of you remember singing along with someone at that piano when you were young?"

Matt's expression shifted from its usual jovialness to one with a touch of sadness. "My grandmother played. We came here for Sunday dinner often. Sometimes we'd stand around the piano and sing afterward."

"His mother was supposed to be a talented musician, too," John added. "I wish I could remember her, but I was too young when she died."

Sandra reached for Matt's hand this time. "Do you remember her at all, Matt? You and John were what? Two when she died?"

"Not quite two. No, I don't really remember her. Just photos and the things my dad and Aunt Kate have told me. I don't have a lot of memories of my grandmother either. I was only five when I lost her." He forced a smile. "Aunt Kate has done a great job filling in for them. Dad, too." He wrapped his arms around John and Sandra. "I'll always miss them, but I'm grateful for the family I have. John really is like a brother to me, and I'm happy to be getting a great sister soon and a little niece or nephew early next year."

~~~

Millie jumped when she heard a car door slam. She looked out the kitchen window and spotted Greg pushing the mower across the backyard. Before she could walk to a front window, someone knocked on the screen door. She hurried across the small living room to the front door, wondering if the week could take any further twists and turns.

When she recognized her visitor, she had her answer. "Good morning, Jeanette. To what do I owe the pleasure of your company?"

Millie unhooked the screen door and pushed it open to admit the harridan. However, Jeanette remained standing on the porch. "I shall stay only a moment, Mrs. Duncan. I came to give you the name of a doctor in Woodbury. I insist on an independent report verifying your daughter is even with child. Once that fact has been confirmed or refuted, then I will proceed with disputing her accusation that my son is the father of her bastard." Jeanette thrust out a hand with a yellow sheet of notepaper clearly ripped from a legal pad with significant vehemence. The top edge was tattered, the bits fluttering in the morning breeze.

Millie slipped her hands into the pockets of her sweater. "We already have a doctor in Woodbury for Sandra to see on Monday. I will be happy to inform you when he confirms you are to be a grandmother. As to any dispute regarding the father of the child, John himself has openly taken responsibility. Sandra assures me he is the only man she has been with, which I did not doubt. They have been in love for two years at least. Mrs. Stuart is satisfied; you are the only one disputing the issue."

In her anger, Jeanette crumpled the paper in her hand. "I certainly am not the only one. None of my friends at the club believe a word of it. My son's reputation shall not be besmirched by your daughter's accusation. He will see sense before this travesty of a wedding can come to fruition. I will not have him marry beneath himself and raise your daughter's bastard as his own."

"Regardless of what you think of my daughter, you will do well not to spread such lies. John is determined to marry Sandra. He loves her, and he knows she is carrying his child. Will you slander your own grandchild before it's even born? Do you have no regard for the innocent babe even if you have none for my daughter or even your son? Who do you think will be most harmed by your gossip when John and Sandra are married and their child is born? You will have failed to stop their union but damaged their reputations and that of the baby. Will you be satisfied then, Jeanette?" Millie grabbed the screen door and pulled it shut with a resounding bang, snapping the hook in place. "I have nothing more to say to you. Please leave this property." She turned her back on the odious woman and stormed off to the kitchen.

~~~

Monday, August 29, 1955

Millie and Sandra entered through the outside kitchen door. Lila shifted her attention from the counter she was cleaning to the ladies. She started to offer to make something for the expectant mother to eat since Sandra had declined both breakfast and lunch before she and Millie left earlier. However, Lila stopped short when she saw the girl's red eyes and downturned lips as she hurried off through the dining room.

"May I get you something for lunch, Millie?" Lila offered.

Shaking her head, Millie said, "Thank you, but no. Maybe later. I need to update Mrs. Stuart and then go check on Sandra." She forced a smile. "Everything's all right. The doctor didn't find any problems and all but confirmed the...diagnosis. We'll get the test results in about a week. She's just a little traumatized from the experience."

"Ah, yes, it's daunting to have someone poking around down there. Certainly, the first time." Lila caught herself. "Well, other than the young man she happens to be in love with."

Millie nodded in agreement. "Speaking of her young man, I didn't see his car or Matt's. Are they both away from the house?"

"Yes, John is running errands for Mrs. Stuart, and Matt is at the stables helping out." Returning to her afternoon ritual, Lila resumed scrubbing the counter. "I expect John will be back soon. He was pacing the floor from the moment you and Sandra left. His grandmother finally made a list of things for him to buy in Elkford and sent him off."

"I'm sure she didn't make his list too extensive. Maybe Sandra will settle down once he returns and they can talk."

Millie followed her daughter's path until she turned down the small hallway leading to the study. To her surprise, the door stood open. She peeked inside and found her employer sitting in one of the chairs in front of the cold fireplace.

Kathryn motioned for her secretary to join her. "Did you and Sandra have any difficulties?"

Settling into the plush, leather chair, Millie closed her eyes and allowed a long sigh to escape. "No, but I wasn't fond of that doctor. Once her pregnancy becomes public, I'm not sure she shouldn't use an obstetrician in Elkford instead of traveling to Woodbury. She doesn't need to rush so far when she goes into labor to be attended by a doctor neither she nor I like. However, it was better to see one there for now."

"Indeed. The gossips will learn of this soon enough, that is, those who aren't already aware, thanks to Mrs. Hathaway and Miss Hathaway. I'm sorry the man wasn't suitable for her. I also agree she needs to plan to deliver in Elkford, not Woodbury. Did he confirm a March date? That would be preferable to winter, but we could still experience weather causing road issues in March and April."

"Yes, late March. Poor Sandra. It was a difficult experience for her."

They heard the front door bang shut, followed by footsteps on the half flight of stairs down to the main floor. Seconds later, they retreated and continued up the staircase to the second level.

Kathryn listened until the sound faded. "It appears John has returned. Perhaps it will settle them both to allow them time alone to discuss the doctor's visit."

"I hope so. They seem to manage well together. I hope that's a good sign for their future."

"Indeed, they do. They must continue to do so, for I fear they will suffer the slings and arrows of many for some time to come with John's mother among the worst offenders."

~~~

Wednesday, August 31, 1955

Three faces peered down at the man in the foyer. A week of relative peace had followed Sandra's move, interrupted only by her obstetrician visit and tidbits related to gossip in Elkford. She had settled into a routine, and her morning sickness continued to improve with the changes to her diet. John had not returned to the Hathaway cottage, and his mother had the good sense not to come to the big house demanding to see him or insisting he return home with her. The big event today would be the interview of the favored candidate to tutor Sandra. The three teens hoped for a peek to allow them to put a face with the name and brief biographical sketch they had of him.

Vance Waters, a retired US Army lieutenant colonel, had taken up education as a second career, but a short stay at Stannum Academy, the state's most elite boarding school, gave him second thoughts. It had taken little to entice him into private tutoring, though he maintained a select clientele. Not one to repeat his mistakes, he would ensure each student he took on would put forth an effort to learn, unlike many of the privileged children at Stannum.

A quiet assurance from his contact in Woodbury led him to accept an appointment at Chestnut Cove to discuss tutoring a young lady who found herself in a delicate condition. A conversation with the Elkford High School principal convinced him Sandra Duncan was bright and eager to learn. Therefore, he agreed to meet her benefactor, whom his contact informed him was the grandmother of Sandra's beau and a force to be reckoned with.

When Lila directed him into the study, Vance found two women awaiting him. The older rose from behind an oak desk and extended her hand. "Colonel Waters, welcome to Chestnut Cove. I am Mrs. Stuart." With a nod at her companion, she continued, "This is Mrs. Duncan, my secretary. Her daughter, Sandra, is to be your pupil should we reach an agreement today. We appreciate you coming here on short notice."

After greeting both women, Vance took the indicated seat across the desk from Mrs. Stuart, and Mrs. Duncan sat in a chair positioned at one end which allowed her to see the faces of both her employer and the prospective tutor. However, the person he felt he most needed to speak to remained absent: the girl.

Once the parties covered Sandra's situation and Vance's qualifications and experience, he said, "Before we proceed further, I would like to meet Miss Duncan, if I may. My discussion with her principal at Elkford High School gave me some feel regarding her aptitude for and attitude toward learning, but I prefer to judge for myself."

"Of course, Colonel. Millie, would you locate her?"

As Millie stood, Vance's lip twitched into a half smile. "I suspect hers was one of three faces I noticed looking down from the floor above when I arrived."

Millie pressed her lips together to maintain a stern visage. "No doubt you are correct, Colonel. I expect I know who the others were, also." She walked around to the bottom of the stairs and looked up in time to catch two heads disappear. "Sandra, come down here and meet Colonel Waters. You might as well come, too, John."

Three heads appeared. "What about me?" Matt whined.

With a roll of her eyes, Millie waved for him to come along, and all three tramped down the steps and followed her into the study. Matt took up a position near the spiral stairs leading up to the library, and John stopped behind Sandra as she came face to face with the imposing man.

Kathryn rose again to make the introductions. "Sandra, this is Colonel Waters. As you know, he is the man we are interviewing to become your tutor. He asked to meet you. Colonel Waters, this is Miss Sandra Duncan. The young man behind her is my grandson and her fiancé, John Stuart." Without turning to acknowledge the third new arrival otherwise, she added, "And the scamp in the corner is my great-nephew, Matt Hunter, who came to live with me after his widowed father moved away for his job.

"All three will be seniors this year, and all are good students. They have access to the library above us as well as any other resources required for their education. Matt particularly excels in mathematics and science. John more so in history, civics, and economics. Sandra is best in English grammar and literature. They frequently study together, which we have found helps all of them to learn better. I hope that situation will be acceptable to you."

Vance nodded his head. "Yes, I find small study groups helpful." He held out his hand and shook Sandra's, then John's. With a glance toward Matt, he added, "I assume your great-aunt does not refer to you as a scamp without reason."

Matt walked across to Vance and shook hands. "Absolutely not. I do my best to live up to my reputation at all times."

Vance allowed his gaze to move from Matt back to John and then Sandra. "Excellent. It isn't good to allow things to become too settled and staid. Assuming Mrs. Stuart and Mrs. Duncan approve of me, I look forward to teaching you, Miss Duncan, and getting to know your friends as well."

Chapter 7

When John went in search of his grandmother the next morning, he couldn't find her anywhere in the house. The previous afternoon, she had provided Millie with a list of errands to handle in Elkford first thing this morning, so the secretary would not be in until close to midday. Matt had gone with Jonah to provide another pair of hands on a couple of small jobs on the estate, and Sandra and Mary were sorting clothes which would soon be unsuitable for the pregnant girl to wear.

John headed into the kitchen to find Lila, source of all knowledge in the Stuart household. "Lila, do you know where Gramma went? I can't find her. She didn't mention going anywhere at breakfast."

Lila pulled her hands out of a sink full of soapy water and began to rinse one of the breakfast plates. "She went out to the carriage house maybe half an hour ago. I expect she's still there."

John's brow contracted. "The carriage house? What's she doing there?" Kathryn's car resided in the lower level of the two-story building situated to the east of the main house with the upstairs used only for storage. "Did she plan to go somewhere in the car?" While capable of driving herself, the elderly lady rarely did so anymore, instead calling upon John, Matt, Millie, or another member of her staff to drive her. "I better go check on her."

He hurried out of the kitchen, through the dining room and hall, and up the stairs to the foyer. Snatching open the front door, he took the steps two at a time and turned left toward the carriage house. He was halfway across the courtyard in front of the mansion when his grandmother appeared at the small entrance on the west side of the carriage house.

"Ah, John, I was about to go in search of you and Sandra." She beckoned for him to approach. "You shall do for now. Come up here with me. Do you remember what the upstairs looks like? It used to provide living space for the coachman and grooms."

"Yes, Matt and I played up here when we were children. It's just storage now, isn't it?" He followed her inside and up the narrow stairway to the second floor.

When they reached the top, she opened the door, which gave access to the small apartment. "Most of what is here needs to be disposed of unless you and Sandra have an interest in it. I intend for you to look through it and select anything you might wish to keep. Then I will ask the minister if he knows of someone at the church in need of anything left."

"Matt, Jonah, and I can move it out of here for you, Gramma, and take it to anyone who needs it."

"Thank you, dear, but that isn't why I wanted you to come up here. Once you and Sandra marry, I believe it would be nice for you to have your own space for a time. While you are welcome to remain in my house, and we can redo the suite of rooms your parents once occupied for you and Sandra to use should you prefer that, I had thought you might like to live here for a time. You and Sandra would be able to set it up as you choose and spend time alone instead of always in the company of your cousin and your old grandmother. It would provide you with a chance to adjust to life as a couple you might not get next door."

John gazed around the apartment. Though small, it consisted of the living room in which they stood, a kitchenette, and a long bunk-type room. "It would be perfect, Gramma. Of course, I need to show it to Sandra and get her opinion, but I would love living here." He pulled the stately woman into a bearhug. "Thank you."

"You are most welcome, dear. Of course, you will be welcome to attend dinner with me and your scamp cousin anytime you wish, but newlyweds deserve their privacy. I expect Sandra will prefer to maintain her own home once you settle here, but I will put Mary at her disposal, also. As her pregnancy advances, she will find herself limited in certain ways. Also, she will require assistance once the baby arrives. I suggest we include a small bed so Millie or Mary or Lila, or even myself, may stay if needed during those first days after Sandra and the baby come home from the hospital."

John could only nod, thoughts of bringing first his bride and then his child into their own home overwhelming him. He could think of no better wedding gift his grandmother could provide them. He finally released her, shifting his attention to the other potential occupant of the apartment. "May I go find Sandra and bring her out here to look at it and ask her opinion?"

"Of course, dear. I believe we should consider making some changes prior to you moving in. The space requires modernization, and I believe it prudent to divide it differently to create two bedrooms. Once you and Sandra have discussed the matter and decided if you would like this for your own, I will call Mr. Pullen to discuss hiring him to make any changes."

"All right, Gramma." He held her hand while they negotiated the stairs and escorted her back into the main house. Racing up to Sandra's bedroom, he stopped in the doorway to watch her hold up one of his favorite dresses and smooth it over her stomach. "Promise me you'll be able to wear that one for months to come."

Sandra smiled at him as she pulled the skirt out. "Maybe a couple of months. Then it will need to go to the back of my closet. Mother is taking me shopping in Woodbury Saturday if I feel all right to buy a couple of things I can wear as the baby begins to show."

"Good, I'm glad you're feeling well enough to consider a trip that far." Remembering his mission, he said, "May I interrupt your work here long enough to show you something and get your thoughts?"

"Of course. Mary needed to go help Lila, so I'm on my own for now. It would be a good time to take a break." He held out his hand, and she took it and allowed him to lead her out the door.

When they reached the carriage house apartment, John informed her of the offer to make it their home once they married. Sandra wandered through the space in shock. "Oh, John, I love it. You know I was nervous about us...sleeping in the same room once we're married right down the hall from your grandmother or Matt. It would be wonderful to have our own little apartment to start our lives together. Assuming we must wait until Christmastime to marry, we would have plenty of time to get this set up to move into. I don't think we would need to have much done to it other than dividing the bunkroom into two separate bedrooms for us and the baby. We could do some work ourselves."

"So, you like it as much as I do?"

She walked back to him and slid her arms up and around his neck. "Yes, it's perfect. I can't wait to live here with you and our little girl or boy." She leaned up on her toes and pressed her lips to his.

~~~

Saturday, September 3, 1955

Scooping up a rock from the edge of the stream, John hurled it across into the trees on the far side of the water. Matt watched in silence from where he lay sprawled on a sandy spot ten feet downstream. John needed to work off some steam, and Matt knew it.

"Mrs. Duncan and Gramma Kate agreed to support us. Why can't Mother?" John grabbed up another stone, worn smooth from years of being worked by the creek, and sent it slamming into the underbrush on the far bank. The previous afternoon, he had returned to his mother's cottage to retrieve his books when she was normally at pinochle, coming face to face with her for the first time in over a week. Their conversation mimicked the previous one, with Jeanette not budging from her position that John would come to see sense regarding Sandra soon.

He kicked at the ground with the toe of his sneaker as he continued to tell Matt about the latest conversation with Jeanette. "She had the audacity to tell me the baby might not even be mine, like Sandra would do...it with other boys. She isn't like that. We love each other and would have married eventually. We just need to sooner than we would have otherwise. I'd have insisted we marry next summer anyway so she could go to Coughton with me." He snatched up a pebble and launched it over the willow gripping the far bank.

Matt rolled over and sat up. "She'll come around, John. She won't have a choice in the end. I know it's hard to wait for her to see reason, but Aunt Kate will win out. She always does. Besides, you'll turn eighteen in December. Even if your mom doesn't change her mind, everyone is working toward the plan for you and Sandra to marry then. She can't stop you from marrying in December."

Before John could start on a rampage about waiting so long, Matt held up his hand. "I know it isn't ideal. None of this is, but Aunt Kate and Mrs. Duncan worked it out for Sandra to be tutored at Chestnut Cove so she can finish high school, and she's living there, too. Aunt Kate's good with you staying there full time now, and your mom can't afford to refuse to go along. If she tries to prevent you living in the big house, Aunt Kate will kick them out of their cottage and make them find a place of their own, and you know they can't afford that. Even if they could, it would take time to find and buy a house of their own. They wouldn't be able to manage it before December."

John leaned his forehead against his knees. "I know, but it's so hard on Sandra. Not that it will be easy even when we're finally married. Mom's old bat friends will talk. They'll probably never accept Sandra, and neither will their children."

"John, we don't hang out with those kids anyway. Don't worry about what they think. Sandra will be fine. You can see she's already feeling better in the last week. She feels so much better she could go shopping with her mother today. She has you, and she has the support of her family and of Aunt Kate. We've got plenty of friends who will stick with us, and it's us, you know. I'm in this with you and Sandra. Anything you need from me, just let me know. I'll even begrudge you naming the baby after me if it's a boy." When John finally raised his head to look at his cousin, Matt grinned in triumph.

"I don't know about that," John drawled, rubbing his chin in his best impression of his late grandfather. "Sandra will have something to say on naming the baby."

"OK, I'll settle for godfather and, of course, best man when you get married."

At last, John allowed his own smile. "Those I can guarantee." He looked around for his pole. "Let's get to catching the fish. I need something to distract me until Sandra and Mrs. Duncan return from Woodbury."

Matt grabbed his own pole and stood. "Want to place a little wager on who catches the most fish?"

Chapter 8

Tuesday, September 6, 1955

John and Matt worked their way through the crowded hallway, greeting friends they had seen little of during the summer. Both were assigned to Mr. Hutchins' homeroom, and when they reached the math teacher's classroom, they found adjacent seats with John behind Perry, one of their friends.

While John and Perry chatted, Matt checked out the other students in the room. Several, including Maria, greeted him. The pair had dated casually a few times and were on friendly terms, but more importantly the girl was one of Sandra's friends. While Sandra continued to remain secluded at Chestnut Cove other than her two trips to Woodbury with her mother, Matt had maintained contact with Maria. She kept him apprised of any gossip she heard regarding Sandra. So far, neither Perry nor any of the boys' friends seemed to know anything.

By lunchtime, Sandra's withdrawal from school was common knowledge among the senior class and to a lesser extent among the lower grades. Matt reached the cafeteria first and was seated among friends when John arrived from the gym. Within seconds of his entry, the din reduced noticeably. He stopped and glared around the room, daring anyone to disparage him or Sandra openly. Matt rose, as did Perry and the other friends at their table. Fortunately, Lila prepared sack lunches for the boys, so John ignored the meal line and wended his way across to where his friends had a seat saved for him.

A gaggle of clucking hens sounded across the room, and Matt took stock of the girls at that table before resuming his seat. "Claudine's friends," he muttered.

"I saw them," John said. "A couple were in biology with me. Talk about awkward. That's going to be my worst class this year."

Talk among the boys shifted to the various cars some of the seniors drove or wished for, their classes, and what they did over the summer. All studiously avoided talk of girls until Perry broached the subject at last. "We heard there was a confrontation between Claudine and Sandra. Your stepsister's crazy, but you know that better than anyone. Claudine got sent back to her mother's? Was Sandra hurt?"

"Mostly she was scared. Thank goodness Greg was there. He got Claudine away from Sandra." He knew Perry had given him an opening to go further and supply the Stuart version of events, so he plunged ahead. "Gramma banned her from Chestnut

Cove, but who knows if that would really stop her. Mrs. Duncan and Gramma decided it would be safer if Sandra moved in with us for now. She keeps a room at both our house and her mother's like I do, but neither of us stays anywhere else now. It's been tense. Gramma thinks it's better for both of us to stay under her roof. She even hired a tutor for Sandra so she can finish school with him instead of here with Claudine's crazy friends." He took a deep breath while he steeled his nerves. "By the way, Sandra and I are engaged. I proposed a couple of weeks ago."

The boys congratulated their friend, and then each took his turn discussing the girls they were dating or had an interest in for the duration of lunch. No one hinted at rumors of a quick wedding date or pregnancy.

<center>~~~</center>

On the way to his next class, Matt saw a clutch of girls cackling in the hall. The mix of juniors and seniors included at least two of Claudine's close friends, Jillian and Rachel. He intended to ignore them, but when he overheard Sandra's name and a couple of outrageous snippets, he veered off the path to physics and shoved his way into the middle of the gathering.

"Good afternoon, girls. Hope you don't mind me barging in. I wanted to let you know about a little thing called slander. In case you're unaware, it concerns intentionally telling lies about people. Claudine has already been kicked out of her father's home for attacking Sandra. She's banned from any Stuart property. We take care of our own, and as I assume Claudine told you, Sandra and John are engaged, which means she's officially part of the family just like we've known she would be eventually. So before you spread any further lies about her, you better consider how long Aunt Kate's reach is when it comes to retribution, and I'm one of her chief assistants. If anyone spreads nasty lies like the one I just heard about Sandra messing around with other guys, I promise you'll think Claudine got off light just being run off. I'm keeping track."

"We're not saying anything you can prove isn't true, Matt," Jillian said. "We know she's knocked up. She sneaks out to a bar over in Inverness and picks up men. I bet she doesn't even know who the baby's father is."

Matt burst out laughing. "At least tell a good lie if you're set on spreading one, Jillian. Inverness is across the county line in Wallace county. It's dry. There are no bars. Besides, it's a tiny crossroads with little more than a general store, a gas station, and a church." He took a pencil from his pocket and flipped open his notebook to a blank page. "J-I-L-L-I-A-N. Congratulations, you're at the top of my list." He grinned down at her. "I'll be sure to tell Aunt Kate what you said. I'm sure she'll tell your parents all about why she'll be using another butcher shop in the future. Losing the Stuart's account won't cause your parents to go out of business, but it sure will hurt. I wonder where they'll go to buy their beef since she probably won't sell to them either?"

"She can't do that!" Jillian shouted. "Besides, who needs your business anyway. It's only you and John and his grandmother."

Matt's grin widened. "And Lila and Mary and all of the people who live and work at Chestnut Cove. None of them will do business with anyone who disparages Sandra or John. We'll buy and sell in Woodbury if necessary. How many people in Woodbury do you think will come to Elkford to buy meat from your father? How much more will it cost him to buy from farther away because Aunt Kate is the biggest beef supplier in Bruce County." He took a step closer to a smirking girl. "All of you need to keep your mouth shut about Sandra and John. None of you is worth a tenth of what she is. She's sweet and smart, and she and John love each other. Unlike the rest of you with designs on him, she doesn't care about his family's wealth. Not one of you is worth a second look from John or me or anyone else. He's lucky to have Sandra, and he knows it."

The bell rang, and Matt pushed his way through to the physics classroom just beyond them, leaving the girls to rush off to their own classes.

<center>~~~</center>

When their children returned to school, the ladies' bridge group at Elkford Country Club resumed its weekly meetings also. A regular since she married first husband Carlisle Stuart in 1935, Jeanette entered the private room prepared to be the center of attention. Between Claudine's calls to her friends and Jeanette's own conversations with a few fellow socialites, Sandra's shame and the sham engagement were well known. Jeanette would milk the horror for all she could.

Paula Dalton already sat at their usual table. Sally sat at the next. She would help keep her group in the conversation with Jeanette's. The Pullen woman, a new club member, had joined Sally. Jeanette couldn't remember her first name. However, a Pullen daughter was a member of Claudine's circle in Elkford, and Sally said the mother showed the proper amount of shock when told of Sandra's plot to trap John. Perhaps the woman would prove herself worthy of her club membership.

Paula took Jeanette's hand and led her to their table. "You look anxious, dear. I so hope an afternoon with your friends will help ease the awful burden you are under." She ushered Jeanette to the chair opposite her own, then took her place at their table. "Have you seen or spoken to John in the last few days?"

"No, not in a week." Jeanette plucked out the handkerchief she had tucked into her sleeve earlier and wiped at her eyes. "It's as if I've lost my only son," she wailed. Not too loud, just enough to attract the attention of those nearest for now. "That awful girl. How could she make such a claim against my poor, sweet, innocent son?"

Another team joined them before Paula could reply, and Jeanette repeated the gist of the story, ensuring she could barely be heard at Sally's table. Soon, the ladies at the adjacent table had pulled their chairs close to commiserate with the sorrowful mother.

"Yes, Mrs. Stuart's secretary's daughter. The woman and the girl have cast some sort of spell over the old bat and my poor son. I'm sure they intend to rob her blind and leave my darling boy destitute. It's bad enough her sister's grandson lives there and mooches off her at John's expense. Now she's moved that girl into the house." A collective gasp escaped the room, though Jeanette had already informed several of the women of that development almost two weeks earlier.

Bridge was forgotten as Jeanette held court. "Well, they claim to have received the test results and confirmed the pregnancy, though no one showed me anything official from a doctor. They refused to see the one I recommended. That speaks for itself. Of course, she may well be in the family way, but I am certain my son would never do such a thing. The girl doesn't come from our kind. There is no telling who the father might be. You know, they have a car, and I believe she's even been allowed to drive one of Mrs. Stuart's cars to run errands helping out at Chestnut Cove during the summer. She could have gone off most anywhere with most anyone."

Matt Hunter's name hung on the tip of Jeanette's tongue, but she exhibited a rare bout of common sense in not invoking him as a potential father. Should word of such a slander get back to the dragon, the wrath would be excessive. The old woman would undoubtedly carry out her threat of evicting her former daughter-in-law from the Stuart estate, like Claudine.

"How could Mrs. Stuart ever allow, much less condone, such a thing?" Mrs. Pullen's exclamation caused her to rise a point in Jeanette's book. Several of the other ladies joined in the commentary and the effort to console the bereft mother.

When the weekly bridge session broke up at five o'clock, not a rubber had been played.

~~~

When Matt parked his 1949 Oldsmobile 88 next to the house, Sandra stood on the kitchen steps waiting for the boys. "How was school?"

Both Matt and John knew the innocuous question held a much deeper meaning. She wanted to know if her withdrawal from school caused a significant stir and how many people suspected or knew she was with child. John stopped and leaned in for a kiss, Sandra at eyelevel with him for once since she remained on the step. "It was OK. At lunch, we caught up with a few of our friends we hadn't seen all summer. We got homework in almost all our classes, mostly reading, though, except math."

Chiming in, Matt said, "Yeah, leave it to Mr. Hutchins to give us a dozen problems to work tonight. How was your first day with Colonel Waters?"

"Fine." She turned and led the boys into the kitchen. "I think I'll like him. He has a broad background and knows quite a lot, and he isn't nearly as imposing as I feared once you get to know him a little. We talked about each class I need to complete to get my diploma. He wants me to take typing, which he doesn't teach, but he knows someone who would come here twice a week for that, and Mother and Mrs. Stuart agreed. Otherwise, I only need English, American history, and another elective to go with typing. We decided introductory bookkeeping would be useful since John will own a business. I should know something about keeping the books so I can help out."

"Enough about school," John said. "How are you feeling? Did you have much morning sickness today?"

"No, almost none. The light breakfasts have really helped." The boys stopped in the kitchen long enough to select an apple apiece before following Sandra through to the veranda. "Colonel Waters arrived at nine o'clock, and we spent an hour each on English and history, took a break, and spent another hour on history. Tomorrow, we'll do bookkeeping for an hour instead of two on history. We finished shortly before one o'clock, he left, and I had lunch with Mother and your grandmother.

"I think that's the pattern we'll stick with except for typing. They're going to let me use the typewriter Mother uses in the study. They plan to set a time with the typing teacher for my lessons and work around that. Mrs. Stuart said it wouldn't be a problem to allow us use of the study for a set couple of hours twice a week. Colonel Waters and I use the parlor for my other classes, so we're not in their way."

Once they seated themselves, Sandra took John's hand and looked directly into his eyes. "Now tell me what they said about me at school. Don't hold back, John." She looked across at Matt, seated on the opposite side of the wrought-iron table. "You, too. I need to know before I run into somebody in Elkford."

John turned pleading eyes toward Matt. He knew Sandra wouldn't be satisfied until she knew, but he couldn't stand to deliver such a blow.

Matt nodded and began, "It's about what you would expect. Claudine's friends got an earful from her either before she got run off to Woodbury or maybe she's keeping in touch with them from there." He hoped Sandra would allow him to stop, but she sat with her eyes locked on him, waiting for more. "They said you got pregnant on purpose to trap John into marrying you. A couple even speculated about the real father's identity."

Sandra's free hand wiped at the tears pooling in her eyes. "Who did they suggest? Anyone I even know?" Her voice broke, making the last words almost indistinguishable.

Matt shook his head. "Nobody at school. I pushed my way into their group and told them how much they disgusted me and how much better a person you are and left." A familiar grin replaced the scowl on his face. "One of the girls was Jillian. I think I finally got her to realize I would never ask her out." The girl had pursued Matt almost as relentlessly and fruitlessly as Claudine had John.

A vision of Jillian's face at what had surely been more pointed and abrupt language than Matt would admit made Sandra smile. "Two good things have already come of this little one." She patted her stomach. "John is free of Claudine's pursuit, and now you're free of Jillian's."

"I hope she got the message," Matt said. "I tried to ensure she and the rest of that crowd understood how I felt regarding what they said about you. If they didn't, I'll be even more direct in the future."

Satisfied with Matt's answer, Sandra shifted the subject to something more pleasant. "Mr. Pullen is coming tomorrow to look at the carriage house. Mary and I walked over there after Colonel Waters left to look around again. The more I think about it, the more I love the idea of us living there one day."

"Why don't we go look at it again this afternoon before we start our homework?" John said. "We'll need to be sure what we want done before Mr. Pullen arrives. We might end up changing if he says it isn't practical, but we need a starting point. We need to make a decision on what furniture to keep, too, so Gramma can let the minister know what she has to donate."

Matt shoved back his chair. "Let's go. I want to make sure you can fit a Matt-sized sofa in your living room for when Aunt Kate gets mad at me and I need somewhere else to sleep."

All three laughed at his suggestion. Kathryn Stuart thought almost as much of Matt as of her grandson. He challenged her in a way no one had since her husband, Alistair, died seven years earlier. She had already lamented losing him, as well as John and Sandra, to college at Coughton Tech the following autumn.

Chapter 9

Wednesday, September 7, 1955

When building contractor Mr. Pullen arrived to survey the carriage house and discuss the changes Mrs. Stuart wanted, he found himself escorted into the building by a parade of women: Mrs. Stuart, her secretary, and the young woman his wife and daughters discussed over dinner the previous night. The reason for the young woman's absence from school for her senior year was an open secret. While Mrs. Stuart only told him she wished for the space to be converted into a home for her grandson and his fiancée when they married, she made it clear the work should be a priority.

As the matriarch enumerated various points he should take into consideration as part of the desired changes, his gaze drifted to the girl. Quite pretty, he thought. He wondered at the easy acceptance by Mrs. Stuart and her grandson that the girl carried a Stuart heir. His daughters indicated they had heard from other friends that Miss Duncan could be quite free with her favors. Perhaps the reason she had been moved into Mrs. Stuart's home was to keep her close at hand and deny her an opportunity to continue keeping company with other boys...or men. After all, since she already carried a child, she couldn't fall pregnant by being intimate with other men. Of course, there would always be opportunities for such a girl to find a way to...get together with someone, and she was very attractive. He licked his lips as he studied her.

"Mr. Pullen."

When he heard Mrs. Stuart's sharp tone, he realized he had become lost in his thoughts. "Yes, ma'am, I'll get right on it." He noticed Sandra and her mother, who had been standing near a window holding their own quiet conversation, turn their attention to the elderly woman. He finally returned his gaze to her also.

"Exactly what is it you will get right on?" Her voice had lost some of its usual rich elegance. Instead, her words came out more clipped and her tone had become low and dark. "I have yet to complete my elucidation of our desired changes, much less come to terms with you for the work." She took a step closer and spoke softly. "I fear you have other things on your mind than my work, Mr. Pullen. While I realize I am not the only person wishing to employ you, I expect your full attention while I inform you of the scope of the job. Clearly your mind is on something other than the work I desire done. Under the circumstances I do not believe I shall waste either my time or yours, now or at any point in the future. Good day, Mr. Pullen."

He had the good graces to look away from her. "Yes, Mrs. Stuart." He managed to keep his eyes trained ahead of him as he retreated down the stairs.

Before he could exit the building, Kathryn Stuart called to him from above. "Please tell your wife I shall not be able to contribute to the fundraiser she is coordinating after all. If she requires an explanation, I shall be pleased to inform her why when next I see her."

He shivered as a chill ran down his back. "Yes, Mrs. Stuart. I understand." Her message had found its mark. He wondered how much business he might lose because of the powerful matriarch's scorn. He vowed to put a stop to his daughters' chatter regarding Sandra Duncan. No doubt the woman would learn who was spreading stories, true or not, about the girl. If Kathryn Stuart began withdrawing business from people who spoke out of turn about her grandson's fiancée, she could do serious harm to a significant number of businesses in Elkford.

~~~

Kathryn led Millie and Sandra back into the house. She offered no explanation to them for her sudden dismissal of Mr. Pullen. Mother and daughter had been too engrossed in their own conversation to notice Mr. Pullen's attention focused unnaturally on Sandra.

"Mary, would you come to the study?" the elderly woman called, her voice penetrating enough to summon the girl from wherever she might be in the mansion.

Kathryn continued into her study, beckoning for mother and daughter to take seats across from her. They heard footsteps on the stairs, no doubt Mary on her way down to attend her employer.

"Yes, Mrs. Stuart?" the young maid said when she poked her head into the study.

"Come in, child. I need a bit of information from you."

"Of course, ma'am. What can I do for you?"

"I have been employing Jonah for several years as a groom in the stables and now as general helper. I understand he has shown an aptitude for determining how to rectify mechanical problems of all sorts. John and Matt think highly of his talent in those quarters." She stopped to allow Mary to acknowledge the praise for her young man.

"Yes, I believe he's considered very talented, Mrs. Stuart."

"He is young but ambitious. He has an interest in one day owning his own construction company?"

"Yes, he does, Mrs. Stuart. It takes money though, and he hasn't saved enough yet for something so bold. He's quite happy for now continuing to work for you and developing his skills."

"Indeed, I am lucky to have him among my estate workers." She steepled her fingertips as she phrased her next statement. "I believe it is time he received the opportunity to show his talent in a more challenging task. I have chosen not to hire Mr. Pullen to do the work necessary on the carriage house. I will assign that task to Jonah. He is patching the roof at the stables this afternoon. Would you take my car– you know where the keys are–and drive down there to inform him I wish to speak to him this evening? Ask him to join us for dinner. Tell your mother to delay her preparations for an hour to allow time for Jonah to change out of his work clothes and join us."

Mary's eyes widened at the implication. "Yes, Mrs. Stuart. Right away, ma'am." She turned to rush off to do as bid but turned back. "Thank you, Mrs. Stuart." She started off again but turned back once more. "Is there anything else, ma'am?"

Kathryn allowed herself to smile. "No, that will be all, Mary. Thank you."

When Mary finally left, Kathryn's eyes shifted to her secretary. "Would you set an appointment for me to meet with my attorney later in the week? I will speak with him about setting up a small construction company for Jonah once he completes the carriage house renovations. If you hear of someone who needs such assistance, I would appreciate it if you would consider referring them to him."

Millie smiled as she reached for the telephone. "Of course, Mrs. Stuart. I would be pleased to tell anyone what a good job he does. I'm sure he'll do well on the carriage house."

While Millie spoke to the attorney's secretary, Kathryn addressed Sandra at last. "I hope this will not cause any friction among you and your friends. You must learn to present clear expectations to those who work for you to ensure there are no misunderstandings. That will limit any hurt feelings later. I believe Jonah will do a fine job with more attention to detail, both because this will be his first such opportunity on something of this scale and because he is a friend to you and John. If all goes as planned, I suspect there will be another wedding in the near future since Jonah should have sufficient funds to marry."

Giddy with happiness for her friends, Sandra said, "I hope so. Mary will be thrilled." She popped up from her chair and ran around the desk to hug the elderly woman. "Thank you, Grandmother Kathryn."

"You're welcome, child, but keep in mind that until I speak to Jonah this evening, you must keep my plan to support him in starting his own business to yourself. Now run along and do your schoolwork before the boys get here. I'm sure you'll have much to tell them."

"Yes, ma'am." She pranced out the study just as her mother hung up the telephone.

Millie noted the appointment on the calendar before she rose and walked to the study door. She glanced out to ensure Sandra was gone before closing it. Resuming her seat, she asked, "Will you tell me what Mr. Pullen did to cause you to send him on his way so abruptly?"

"No, but I imagine you already suspect why. I shall handle it, Millie, with a little assistance from another quarter. Don't worry about it. Now, let us turn our attention to other matters of business."

~~~

When John and Matt arrived home from school, Sandra gave them a brief summary of the afternoon's events as she escorted them into the house. Millie had left early to run another errand for Kathryn, and Lila and Mary were in the kitchen working, or at least Lila was.

Mary could hardly contain her excitement. Though Mrs. Stuart had not specifically told her she planned to provide financial backing for Jonah to open his own business, she had no doubt that was the intent assuming he did well on the carriage house modifications. As usual when there would only be the immediate family for dinner, Mary and Lila would join them in the dining room to eat. Today, Jonah would, too.

The boys and Sandra made their usual stop in the kitchen to find something to snack on, more so today since dinner would be delayed by an hour. As they entered the great room, Kathryn stood in the door of the hall leading to the study.

"Matt, I require a short discussion with you." Not waiting for a response, she retreated to the study to await him.

After a quick glance at John and Sandra, he obeyed the summons. Upon entering, he closed the door without being bid to do so. Whatever the subject, it would require privacy.

"Have I done something wrong, Aunt Kate?" He took a seat without waiting for her to direct him to a chair.

Her eyebrows raised, she said, "I suspect you have, though I am unaware what it might be this time."

Matt's toothy grin flashed into view. "Good. As long as you don't know, whatever it is won't hurt you."

"I should hope not." The corner of her mouth twitched, but otherwise she showed no sign of a smile. "I have a task for which you are uniquely suited. I expect you already know I did not hire Mr. Pullen as planned today."

Matt nodded slowly, his mind racing ahead. "Sandra and Mary couldn't stop talking about you asking Jonah to do the work. I take it you will assist him in starting his own business assuming he does a good job on the carriage house?"

"Yes, and I fully expect him to do an exceptional job. However, what I require from you does not involve that, though you may also be asked to provide an able pair of hands on occasion as you and John often do when needed."

"Of course, Aunt Kate. I'll be happy to help when Jonah needs crew for toting and lifting, but you want my help related to the reason you didn't hire Mr. Pullen?"

"Indeed. I have reason to believe he has heard unfounded gossip regarding Sandra. He has two daughters at Elkford High School, does he not?"

Matt's eyes narrowed. "Yes, one a junior and one a freshman. The older one is a friend of Claudine's. One of her closest friends, I believe, and among the group I confronted yesterday. Someone needs to make a further effort to squelch gossip from that quarter? Or, failing their ability to learn not to believe or spread such rumors, needs to be taught a lesson?"

The crinkle around her eyes provided her response. "I will see to the mother. I already ensured Mr. Pullen understood I would do so should she participate in such rumormongering. You may be aware she and her husband are recent members of the country club. I understand she joined the ladies' bridge group, so she is at least an acquaintance of Jeanette's, if not a friend. I expect the man to make some effort to control his daughters, but I don't know how successful he will be. I want them handled by someone I am sure can and will get our point across by whatever means necessary."

"Don't worry, Aunt Kate. I'll take care of them. It will be my pleasure."

Chapter 10

Sunday, September 11, 1955

"I felt like everyone was staring at me," Sandra whispered. She and John sat close in the back of Kathryn's Lincoln Cosmopolitan with Matt behind the wheel and the matriarch seated beside him in the front.

"Just ignore them," John replied. "I tried to picture what it will look like when you're walking down the aisle toward me in a puffy white dress." He pressed his lips to her temple, hoping to ease the tension he could feel in her muscles.

"I was picturing Greg trying to remember where to stand once he passes you off to John at the altar like at Cindy and Cal's wedding," Matt said with a laugh. "At least he's experienced in giving away a sister now. Maybe he won't be as nervous. I need to remind him of that at dinner." He took a quick look in the rearview mirror. Millie's car trailed her employer's by a short distance as they returned to Chestnut Cove after church.

"Gramma," John said, "have you decided when to approach Reverend Walker about the wedding?"

Kathryn turned to face John and Sandra. "We want to finalize just what the two of you desire and have an agreement as to what we would settle for if we cannot entice the reverend to consent to everything. I do not foresee a significant problem since you've indicated you only wish for a small ceremony of mostly family. You are still certain you only desire Cindy to stand up with you, Sandra?"

"Yes, ma'am, and Mary will help with the bridal book and pour the punch. My dress and Cindy's will cost enough. At least Greg can wear the same suit he wore for Cindy's wedding. Mother might want a different dress than she wore at Cindy's, but she uses them for church afterward. Greg can wear his suit on Sundays, too."

"Sandra, I've already told you not to concern yourself with the cost of anything related to the wedding. I am happy to cover those expenses. I want you and John to have the ceremony you desire. This is something you do only once. My gift to you shall be to ensure it is a day you remember fondly for years to come."

"I appreciate that, Grandmother Kathryn, but we're not an extravagant family. I'll be happy with a simple dress and small wedding."

Seeking to shift the subject away from money, Matt asked, "Have you decided about inviting a few of our friends from school? Just a few select ones like Maria and

Perry who we've all been close to for a long time. They already know about the baby and have jumped in to defend you."

"I'm not sure. We've talked about it, and I really appreciate their friendship. We need to make a list. Matt, would you ask Maria to call me if it's all right with her parents? Some might not want their children associating with me now, so I don't want to call them and get them into trouble."

"I'll do better than that. I'll call her after dinner and ask her if it's OK with her parents. If so, I'll hand you the phone so you can talk to her."

Sniffling softly, Sandra said, "Thank you, Matt."

"Anytime, cousin-to-be."

They reached the turn to enter the cove, and Matt drove across the narrow bridge which served as the primary conduit in and out of the estate. The wrought-iron gates stood open in welcome. The car wound through the trees until it reached the rock promontory where the Stuart home perched. Below, a herd of cattle grazed. Soon, they would be culled to reduce their numbers before winter set in. Kathryn Stuart had held a terse conversation with one local butcher days earlier to inform him he would need to look elsewhere for beef. Two others were happy to split what would have been the first's share.

The smell of a pork roast wafted through the house when they entered. Lila had left one in the oven earlier. She and Mary would return shortly from their own church and complete dinner preparations.

"Let's work on the wedding list while we wait for Mary and Lila," Matt said. Not waiting for a response from anyone, he walked to the study to gather pen and notepad. When he returned to the great room, he sat and began to list the family members. "All right, Sandra and John and Cindy and Greg and I make up the official wedding party. Then there's Millie and Calvin and Aunt Kate and my dad." He stole a quick look at John. "Jeanette and Winston, too, I assume. No Claudine. Anyone else who qualifies as family?"

"No, not from mine," Sandra said. "Right now, we'd have almost as many people standing up front with the minister as sitting in the pews."

"Well, then there's Mary and Lila and Jonah. Are we including the rest of the staff?"

"We've known most of them for years and think a lot of them," John said. "Lila, Mary, and Jonah are closest, but I'd be happy to invite the rest, too. We work out in the fields and in the stables and dairy with them." He heard the front door open and close before Millie and Greg entered to join the group.

Kathryn acknowledged them before replying, "I would be happy for you to invite any of my staff. You still wish to hold a reception here after the wedding instead of in the church fellowship hall?"

Sandra looked around the great room, considering how many people would comfortably fit. "If it isn't too much an imposition, Grandmother Kathryn. The house will already be decorated for Christmas, and we discussed combining the reception with your normal staff gathering before Christmas. Is that still acceptable to you?" She had attended the festivities each year her family lived on the estate but never considered the logistics of the event.

"Indeed, it is quite a nice idea. We shall simply include any wedding guests outside the Chestnut Cove staff this year. Perhaps you would like to have another gathering of your friends during the holidays, also. Something specifically for the young people?"

"I wouldn't want to impose or create more work."

Lila had entered from the dining room and replied for her mistress. "Nonsense. I don't often get to cook for more than a handful of people anymore. This house is bursting with joy to be adding young people after so long, even that young scamp." She pointed at Matt with the meat fork she held. "Now, I need someone to help carry food into the dining room."

"I didn't even know you and Mary were back," Matt said, setting aside his list and standing. "I'd have been in to help already otherwise." The rest of the group rose also, and soon they all sat around the table enjoying Lila's feast and discussing the wedding.

~~~

Tuesday, September 13, 1955

Rachel Pullen peeked out from under fluttering eyelashes as the football players hustled out to practice. She and her friends had stationed themselves close to the gymnasium door to show off their assets in their new gym uniforms. Rachel paid particular attention to the senior quarterback. She had her sights set on him as her date to the first dance of the fall, though a number of other girls did also.

To ensure they could remain close until the team returned from the practice field, she and her friends volunteered for the spirit team. They would change back into their finery and paint signs after school during the weeks of home games. The painstaking effort would coincide with football practice each day. An unfortunately-timed dental appointment forced Rachel to miss the previous day's festivities. She determined to make up ground today.

Later in the afternoon, the sound of male voices stirred activity among the gossiping group of girls. To the disappointment of most, the cross-country team wandered out of the locker room. The small group of boys consisted of two freshmen, three sophomores, a junior, and a senior.

Normally keen to attract the attention of any senior, Rachel feigned disinterest when the team leader winked at her. Matt Hunter had let it be known he supported his cousin and the little slut who had captured him, putting him square at the head of those supporting the illicit couple. Still, he was cute and well-connected if not wealthy like his cousin.

When he stopped to chat up a cheerleader, Rachel felt a stab of jealousy. Matt had held the cafeteria door open for the elder Pullen sister and a friend last Friday. He smiled at her, too. She strained to hear bits of his conversation with the cheerleader, but the pair spoke in animated whispers. Matt shook his head and moved off, chatting with another girl as he walked along the wall where the banner they just finished painting waited to be hung.

"Matt," a third girl called, "would you help us put this one on the wall? We need someone taller to help us. The paint is still wet, so we have to be extra careful with it."

"Sure." He set his gym bag on the bleachers and walked back across to a spot near Rachel. "How about if I stand here in the middle while you girls work your way out with the tape?"

"That would be great, Matt," the girl replied.

Matt took position and lifted the center of the long banner while a couple of the girls held each end. Rachel moved up to place tape near Matt and remained there as the others worked their way to the ends.

"All done?" he asked when it appeared the girls had completed their mission.

"Yes, thanks, Matt," several answered.

He backed away as if trying to take in the enormity of the artwork. "Oh, sorry," he said as he bumped into Rachel. He moved back toward the wall, though careful not to touch the sign.

She smiled up at him. "It's quite all right. No harm. Thank you for helping us, Matt." Competition for the quarterback would be fierce for Friday night's dance, and Matt was awfully cute. Surely John wouldn't attend with his pregnant slut, so Matt wouldn't feel he needed to express support for them during the evening. She batted her eyes and closed the distance between them to only a step. "The cross-country team practices every afternoon just like the football team, doesn't it?"

Matt's eyes sparkled at her. "Yes, we do." He spoke softly as he gazed into her eyes. He extended one hand to strike a casual pose propped against the wall, though careful that his hand touched only the dry, white part of the paper sign. "Do you like track and field sports? Most girls are only interested in football stars." His voice had dropped to an intimate whisper.

Rachel inched closer. "Oh, I love it. It's so exciting to watch you jump over those wooden things."

"Ah, yes, jumping those wooden things is tricky." He pushed off the wall and positioned himself between her and the rest of the gym. He stuck his hands in his pockets and kicked at the floor with his foot. "So, Rachel, are you going to the dance Friday?" He spoke so low no one else could possibly hear him.

She dipped her head and peered up through her eyelashes. "I was considering it, but I haven't decided." Then she leaned back against the wall. "Are you going, Matt?"

Straightening, he spoke at an amplified volume. "No, I'll be out of town at a cross-country meet. Besides, I'd *never* go out with somebody who spreads despicable lies about two of my closest friends like you've done. By the way, we don't jump over those wooden things, which are called hurdles, in cross-country." He turned away and stormed over to grab his bag on his way out of the gym, leaving the girl in stunned silence.

"Rachel," someone yelled, "you're messing up the sign!"

Staring at the door Matt disappeared through, it took several seconds for Rachel to comprehend the totality of the situation. When it sank in, she shrieked and jumped away from the wall. "No!" She spun and saw the smeared paint where she had leaned against the sign. She tried to look over her shoulder to see the damage to the back of her blouse and skirt, spinning like a dog chasing its tail. The football team chose that moment to surge into the gym. Howls of laughter erupted from them at the spectacle of the gyrating, paint-covered girl. She burst into tears and ran out the far end of the gym.

~~~

Matt parked beside John's car when he arrived home. Jonah and John stood at the back of Jonah's truck, which held a load of lumber and pipe.

John waved him over to join them. "Hey, Matt, how was practice?"

"Not bad. The freshmen are all pretty good. We should have a decent team this season." He scanned the contents of the truck. "Getting started on John and Sandra's apartment already, Jonah?"

Wiping sweat from his face with a stained handkerchief, Jonah shook his head. "No, got another roof to help repair first and some fence, but I spent much of the day buying material and gathering the supplies I'll need. When he got home, John and I moved the furniture they plan to use downstairs. Don't want it in danger when I'm working."

"Got more to move? I can help now."

"Oh yeah," John said with a laugh. "Now we need to unload the truck. We made space to store the material inside. We also need to move the things Reverend Walker said someone can use and load them on the truck. Jonah is taking that to the church tomorrow before rain moves in later this week. Going to be a soggy game Friday night. I hope your cross-country meet won't get too much."

"Let me go in and change into my overalls. I'll be right back." He snagged his gym bag and books from his car and raced inside and up to his third-floor bedroom.

When he came back down, he continued past the foyer and down the half flight of steps and around the corner to the study. Millie's car wasn't here, so he knew his aunt should be alone. He tapped on the door and entered when bid to do so. "I need to get back to help Jonah and John, but I wanted to let you know I completed my assignment this afternoon. I'll keep an eye out to ensure it sticks, but the older Pullen girl won't forget this afternoon's lesson anytime soon."

Kathryn smiled up at him. "Excellent. I knew I could count on you, dear."

He gave his commanding general a quick salute and raced outside.

"Grab those boxes of plumbing and electrical fittings in the cab," Jonah called. He and John held each end of a stack of lumber, carefully maneuvering it into the carriage house.

Matt opened the truck door and stacked the boxes before lifting them out, pressing his chin on the top of the pile to hold them steady. He trailed John and Jonah up the stairs and set the boxes in a corner. "Don't we need to take more downstairs before we bring more up?"

"Yep," John replied, "we have enough space opened up now that we can carry one load up and another down. We'll get this sofa. You grab that end table."

They set their burdens on the driveway next to the truck and repeated the process. When they returned with the next load, they found Sandra and Mary had utilized the small table to hold a tray containing a pitcher of lemonade and several glasses. Matt rolled his eyes in mock disgust as Jonah and John greeted their ladies with exaggerated enthusiasm. He picked up the pitcher and began to fill the glasses. "My work is never done," he mumbled.

When he lifted one glass to partake of the refreshment at last, John grabbed it from him and took a long drink. "Thanks, Matt." He laughed at his cousin's expression.

"This is the treatment I get? The thanks I get for all I do for you? I should have taken Rachel up on going to the dance Friday night."

"Rachel? Claudine's friend? You can't stand her," Sandra exclaimed. "Besides, you'll be out of town at a meet Friday."

"Oh, but Rachel and I had a moment together this afternoon. I don't think she fully understood me until then." His mouth twisted into a fierce grin. "She does now."

When Lila located the group to let them know dinner would be served shortly, she found them lounging on the furniture arranged on the driveway as if adorning the great room inside the mansion. The empty pitcher and glasses sported sprigs of greenery and the earliest of the autumn leaves exhibiting tinges of orange and yellow. The truck, emptied of its earlier burden, waited for the outdoor playhouse to be packed into its bed.

Chapter 11

"Does it hurt much? Can you manage the steps?"

Matt waved Sandra off. "They just want me to be careful of it a few days. I can go down the stairs holding onto the bannister." He tucked the crutches under one arm and eased down the half flight to the bottom. Once safely back on a flat surface, he tucked the wooden aids under his arms and made his way to the nearest overstuffed chair. He snagged an ottoman with the tip of a crutch and guided it closer to his chair and propped up his injured foot.

"Do you need some ice to put on it? I can get some for you."

"You'll make a fine mother, Sandra, but no, I don't need a thing except a less slippery course to run on." He waved for her to sit. "Where is everyone? It isn't like John to leave you here unguarded."

She finally perched on an adjacent chair. "Lila and Mary are in the gatehouse. They'll be back in here soon. I'm sure they heard you come in and would have come right over if it had been someone else. John went with Jonah to haul some of the old material he tore out of the carriage house to the dump. They only left half an hour ago, so it will be some time before they return. Mrs. Stuart went to the country club."

Matt's eyebrows rose. "Really? She rarely does that anymore. Was there some meeting or special event?"

"I don't know. Someone called earlier. When she got off the phone, she had Gus come up to the house to drive her." She watched Matt, waiting to see how he reacted.

"Uh oh, that sounds like she's on the warpath. Could you hear her on the phone? Did she answer or Lila or Mary?"

"Mary. I thought about asking who called, but I don't think I should pry."

Chuckling, Matt replied, "You're a saint. Don't worry, I'll find out as soon as Mary or Aunt Kate returns." He shifted to get more comfortable. "Now, tell me about the carriage house apartment progress. Jonah finished taking down that old wall? I hope nothing else on the estate happens to delay work on it. He's excited to get to do that for you and John as well as to show his talent to Aunt Kate. It seems like everything on the estate has conspired to drag him away to help the rest of the crew. At least he's finally been able to spend a couple of days on your apartment."

She broke into a smile, something of a rarity for the last month. "Oh, it looks so different with that bunkroom wall gone. Mary and I went up to see it once Jonah and John got the debris out. It seems much larger right now. Of course, that will change again once he builds the new walls for our room and the nursery."

"I won't try to go up today, but I should be getting around better tomorrow. I'll look then. I want to make sure you have room for a Matt-sized sofa. If Jonah got mad at me for something, he might shift a wall just enough to ensure it won't quite fit."

Sandra laughed at the thought. "No, he wouldn't. He would never do such a thing, and you know it." She wiped at her eyes with a tissue. "You've dodged the issue enough. Tell me what happened to your ankle."

"A hazard of running cross-country: a snake."

"A snake? It didn't bite you, did it? I know you don't panic when you see one. What happened?"

"No, it was just a little rat snake, but one of the freshmen from Woodbury High probably never spent any time in the country, and he panicked when it crawled across the course. He stopped and jumped sideways right in front of me. I tried to dodge him, and my foot landed on some loose gravel to the side of the path. I ended up wrenching my ankle. Like I told you, it's nothing serious, but coach wants me to stay off it as much as I can tonight. It's just a little sore. We iced it right away. That helped."

"Do you want to sleep down here tonight? You keep fussing about us having a sofa for you in case Grandmother Kathryn gets mad at you. She has one you could sleep on right here if you don't want to deal with climbing all the way to the third floor tonight. I can get you a blanket and pillow."

"Mmm, maybe. Depends on how it feels later. John can help me get up without putting much weight on it, and I got down to this floor from the foyer without a problem. I need to make it to church tomorrow morning, too. I have that solo part to do." Shifting the topic away from his ankle, he continued, "Oh, tomorrow evening you and John have your first session with Reverend Walker, and this will be the first time we've been to church since Aunt Kate and your mother settled the wedding date and time with him. Are you nervous about talking to him?"

She sighed and scrunched up a little in her chair. "Yes. At least John will be there. Mother told me about going through it when she and Dad married, too. I don't think it would bother me normally." She put her hand on her stomach. "But obviously we know each other..." Her cheeks pinked and she stopped.

"Better than some couples do before marriage? Or at least better than some admit?"

She nodded, nibbling on her lower lip. "Yes, we can't deny that."

"Sandra, don't worry about it. This time next year, you'll be happily married to John, and I'll be fussing over my godson or goddaughter and all this will be behind you."

"I know, and you're right. I'm sure it will be better once we've completed the first session with him and know what to expect."

Further discussion ended when they heard the front door open and shut. Then six deliberate steps descended to the main floor. Kathryn entered the room and came to a sudden halt. "How bad is it?"

"Just a minor sprain," Matt said. "The crutches are a precaution. I should be fine in a day or two. Coach probably won't let me run at practice Monday to be safe, but I won't escape it any longer than that. Now quit dodging the more important issue. Sandra said you went to the club. Someone required a lesson?"

"Yes. It's been dealt with."

"Uh oh. Jeanette?"

She shook her head. "No, one of her friends." She turned her attention to Sandra. "How are you feeling, dear?"

"Fine, Grandmother Kathryn. I've had much less nausea and more energy the last few days. I hope that means I'm almost over this phase of my pregnancy."

"That's a good sign. You'll feel much more like dealing with your schoolwork and planning the wedding. When we both have free time over the next few weeks, I would like to begin to familiarize you with some of the estate business. I've done so with John for several years to assist him in the eventual transition to managing it. You should become aware of some details also. It is much better to learn small things and build upon that knowledge over time than to be thrust into it upon my death or some serious illness. You're bright and will learn rapidly as has John, and your mother will be a help one day because she has learned much as my secretary."

Sandra's eyes widened into saucers. John had mentioned that his grandmother would eventually wish to teach Sandra about the estate, but she hadn't expected it so soon. On top of everything else, the suggestion she would be responsible for managing the house and possibly other parts of Chestnut Cove came as a daunting task. However, she knew she was smart and a quick study, and John would be there to support her. "Yes, Grandmother Kathryn. I'll be ready when you wish to teach me, and I'll do my best to live up to your standards."

~~~

Thursday, September 29, 1955

The phone on her employer's oak desk rang, and Millie stopped typing at her small table to walk across to answer. "Stuart residence, may I help you?" She picked up a pencil to write down any necessary information.

"This is Mr. Michaelson's office. He would like to speak to Mrs. Stuart regarding the country club lease issue."

Millie jotted down the time in the call log she maintained. "She is unavailable at this time. I will let her know he called." The secretary on the other end acknowledged the response, and Millie replaced the receiver in its cradle. "Mr. Michaelson's office again about the country club lease."

Kathryn Stuart looked up from the ledger in front of her. "He is very determined. I have told him I will not reopen the matter. I wonder how long it will take him to accept that and understand all his machinations to oust the previous chairman and the director are for naught, at least on that subject."

"I hope he will accept it soon. His secretary doesn't seem to have caught on that you are never home to take his calls."

"No, I gather intelligence is not the quality he most seeks in a secretary." Kathryn set aside her reading glasses. "I wonder how his new wife will tolerate it, for I understand she is bright, so she cannot remain unaware for long. I know her family and cannot understand why they allowed her to marry such a man. Detestable in his business conduct and worse elsewhere." She stood and walked across to stand in front of the glowing fireplace. "You know he and Winston Hathaway attended Stannum Academy together?"

"I knew some connection existed. They don't strike me as compatible enough to be close friends."

"No, whatever his character flaws, Vaughn Michaelson is a shrewd man, very intelligent. Mr. Hathaway is simply a gluttonous, slothful fool, which is why he decided to trade his first wife for my former daughter-in-law. He should have taken more time to realize Jeanette had no claim upon the Stuart estate beyond whatever she may extract from John one day. Two more foolish people I've never seen. They deserve one another. I only wish John and Sandra could be spared the pair."

Millie smiled at the mention of her future son-in-law and daughter. "You've taught him well, Mrs. Stuart. He won't allow his mother to manipulate him enough to do any damage. He loves her, as any son should, but he also knows her well enough by now to be wary of her schemes."

"Yes, and I hope he will learn to apply that to other people." She returned to her desk and eased down into her chair. "I fear Mr. Michaelson will be an issue to be dealt with for years to come. I must speak to John about the man. If I had realized how ruthless he is earlier, I believe I would have reconsidered renewing the country club's lease at all. They could purchase land to build anew at a decent price in the current market."

"Yes, ma'am, but the members seem too set on tradition, if I may say so."

"You are correct. The club has been on that site from its establishment around 1919. Alistair sold them the land originally, and he held the mortgage because he would give them a better rate than the bank. After all, we began the club along with our friends and business associates and wanted it to succeed."

"The stock market collapse in 1929 led to the change?"

"Yes, the club couldn't afford its mortgage payments by early 1930 because several members lost money and resigned. Alistair agreed to cancel the mortgage and lease the property for twenty-five years at a minimal rate. The extension of that lease is what we renegotiated this spring. As a member of its board, Mr. Michaelson objected, insisting I set a price for the club to purchase the land. However, the majority declined to meet my sale terms, so we renewed the current arrangement for another twenty-five years at an increased rate.

"Now that he has ousted those with whom I negotiated, he wants to revisit the matter. I, however, will not consider doing so with that man under any circumstances. Simply a detestable human. I hope he is long gone before John must deal with the matter in another twenty-five years. Perhaps Matt will remain here and go into business with John. I adore my grandson, but I believe Matt would be more ruthless in dealing with such people when necessary."

"I believe he inherited a little more of what you call the McDougal temperament than John," Millie said.

"Indeed, my sister, his grandmother, carried the family banner in that respect. He is also a little shrewder and more wary of others' motivations than John." Tapping her pencil on the desk, she continued, "I must do more to encourage him to return to

Elkford once he completes his education and spends some time in military service. He is quite determined on that point, though I have hope of convincing him to follow a slightly different path." Her eyes shifted focus. "Millie, remind me to write to a friend in Washington, actually a military associate of Ian, my late elder son. I wish to understand more about the organization by which he is now employed. He retired from the military three years ago. He now works at a government agency based in Washington, DC, for which I believe Matt would do well to join after college. I would like to present him information regarding this option before he commits to military service."

"Yes, Mrs. Stuart, I'll make a note." She picked up a pad with a list of tasks for her employer to undertake.

Chapter 12

Friday, October 7, 1955

When Matt and John got home, they found Colonel Waters, Jonah, and Gus with their heads under the hood of Millie's 1947 Fleetline. An array of parts littered a canvas tarp on the ground. The boys abandoned their books and gym bags to join the fray.

John leaned in between Jonah and Colonel Waters. "What's wrong with it?"

"'Fraid it's a goner," Gus said. "We pulled the head and found pieces all down inside. We're trying to see if it's worth putting a new engine in it or not."

Matt got down on the ground and scooted under the front. "Got a lot of wear in the steering linkage. These windy mountain roads are hard on it."

Sandra had heard the boys drive up, and she and her mother walked outside to learn of any updates on the prognosis.

Millie's tension showed in her face. A car was not in her budget this year. "Well, do you have a verdict? Is there any way to salvage it?"

It was Vance Waters who spoke for the group. "You could replace the motor, Mrs. Duncan, but it would cost more than the car would be worth to do so. It has too much wear on other parts."

John walked over and put an arm around his future mother-in-law. "Matt and I can share one of our cars for now and let you drive the other. You don't need to buy something in a hurry and not get a good deal."

"Thank you, John. I might take you up on your offer for a short time, but I cannot impose on you for more than a few days." She rubbed her hands up and down her arms. "I'll manage something. For now, we need to get this out of Mrs. Stuart's driveway. I'll call a junkyard to come get it on Monday morning."

Colonel Waters cleared his throat. "If I may, Mrs. Duncan, I know someone who might make you a better deal for the body and chassis than most of the local junkyards. If you will allow me, I could call and describe the car and solicit an offer for you. You would be under no obligation to accept it, of course."

"That would be very kind of you, Colonel. Thank you. I'd also like to thank you for remaining here this afternoon to help Gus and Jonah with it."

"It was my pleasure, Mrs. Duncan."

"Colonel Waters," Kathryn called from the porch where she had come out to survey the efforts to save Millie's car. "I would like to extend an offer for you to remain a little longer today and dine with us. You have been most kind in providing assistance. Offering you dinner is the least we can do."

"Yes, Colonel, please stay," Millie echoed. She smiled at him and felt her cheeks flush slightly.

"Yeah," Matt chimed in. "I'll go pick up Greg from Millie's. We just dropped him off on the way home from school. We can have a big family meal tonight." Without waiting for anyone to respond, he hopped in his car and took off for the Duncan cottage.

~~~

What began as a slightly stiff meal soon relaxed somewhat into the normal family dynamics with Colonel Waters added to the mix. He and the boys discussed cars, and each had suggestions for what Millie should purchase.

Kathryn sensed her secretary's unease and steered the conversation toward school. "Colonel, we were pleased with your report that Sandra is doing well in her studies and is ahead of where you expected in each area. With the distractions she has suffered in the last month, such progress reflects well on you both."

"Thank you, Mrs. Stuart. I've found her to be a superior student. She will make a formidable partner for your grandson in the future." Turning his attention to John, the colonel continued, "Do you know what you will study at college next fall, John?"

"General business seems the logical thing, and I believe I would enjoy learning accounting and marketing. I know a little from working with Gramma. I hope Sandra will decide to attend, too. She'll be living there, so it wouldn't be much extra for her to take classes."

Sandra shrugged. "I might later, but I think it will be a lot to handle learning to be a wife and setting up our apartment in the carriage house. Then we'll have the baby, and I'll need to learn about being a mother. Next fall, we'll have to get all three of us settled into an apartment in Coughton for the school term. Adding college classes is more than I want to consider for now."

"What about you, Matt?" Colonel Waters prompted. "You plan to attend Coughton, also?"

"Yes, sir," Matt replied. "I plan to major in mathematics. I've been told I'm very good at working through problems, both math and others, and it would help me hone those abilities. After I graduate and spend a few years in the military, I can get a job in a technical field or go on to law school or something like that where figuring out details is important."

"You run cross-country in high school. Any plans to continue that at college?"

"No, I don't think so. It's fun, but I believe I'd prefer to investigate other experiences college will offer and not tie myself to athletics."

"Do you play any sports at school, John?"

"I played basketball in the past, but I decided not to do that this year. By the time the season ends, it will be close to Sandra's due date, and I don't want anything to interfere with being here for her. I almost pushed to drop out at Elkford and let you tutor me along with Sandra, but Gramma and I discussed it and she talked to the principal and ensured they would let me stay in school even after we get married in

December." He shifted back in his chair, trying to contain his aggravation. "It isn't fair I'm allowed to stay at Elkford High, but Sandra wasn't."

Sandra set her fork on her plate and put her hand over John's. "We've talked about that. It's all right. There's no way I could stay. This way, I'll be able to resume my studies as soon as I recover from giving birth. I couldn't do that at school even if they let a pregnant girl attend for part of the year. It's worked out well this way. Colonel Waters doesn't teach biology and the advanced math you're taking this year. You shouldn't miss out on those. I'm pleased Grandmother Kathryn convinced them to let you stay the whole school year."

"Still not fair," John grumbled.

After dinner, Matt handed his keys to Millie. "Remember, she's got more power than your Chevy had. Take it easy."

"Thank you, Matt," Millie answered, giving his hand a little pat. "I'll take good care of it. I hope to find something to buy next week, so I won't need it long."

"Keep it as long as you need to," Matt said.

"How about I follow you home to make sure you don't have a problem with it, Mrs. Duncan?" Colonel Waters offered.

Millie smiled and blushed, something that had become too commonplace today. "Thank you, Colonel. I'd feel better with someone following me while I get used to it."

As he trailed her and Greg out the front door of the house, he replied, "Please, call me Vance."

~~~

Saturday, October 8, 1955

"I am at my wits end with them both." Jeanette's fork waved around as she ranted loud enough for anyone at the east end of the Elkford Country Club's dining room to hear. "John will not even consider the girl might be lying, and his grandmother must be senile and under the power of that secretary woman. Between mother and daughter, they have established control over the remnants of the Stuart family." The fork jammed into the cake on her plate. "I simply do not know what other recourse is left to me." A generous portion of cake disappeared into her mouth when Jeanette required further fuel for her ravings.

"Oh, my dear, Jeanette," Paula Dalton said. "I cannot imagine how you sleep at night. And poor Claudine. She remains in Woodbury with her mother?"

"Yes, and I have no expectation she shall return to Elkford. She and John were becoming close before this...thing happened, or rather that girl claimed it did so. Poor Claudine was stricken at the loss; she simply cannot stand to stay with us knowing John has fallen under the sway of that little tart. How can my poor boy think of marrying such a girl?" Cake forgotten, she raised her napkin to dab at her eyes, staining it with a liberal amount of tan and black.

Paula patted her friend's hand. "Perhaps he'll see sense before it's too late. He must wait until his eighteenth birthday. Even his grandmother lacks the power to change the law in that regard. You must remain strong and not give in to allow an earlier marriage. Much may happen in two months. He could see her as you do before December."

Jeanette snorted in disgust. "The old dragon and the tramp's mother made wedding arrangements two weeks ago without bothering to consult me. I only learned about it this week. The pastor agreed to marry them—in the church, no less—on December twenty-third. I spoke to him about it, but he said John and the girl have already begun attending the marriage preparation classes. The minister believes they are very mature for their age. Most compatible, he called them, too. Can you imagine? The Stuart heir compatible with such a common guttersnipe?"

The volume of the last comment interrupted the conversation between Winston and Paula's husband, Hoyt. "Jeanette," Winston spoke sharply, "keep your voice down. Do you want everyone to know?"

"Everyone already knows, and they should. Perhaps the ruination of the girl's reputation will convince John to give up this nonsense. I still want proof she is even with child, much less that it must be John's."

Further dispute between the Hathaways ended for the moment when Vaughn and Lilly Michaelson stopped at the table. "Good evening, my friends," Vaughn drawled. "I hope you are having a pleasant dinner. I didn't see you in the clubhouse today, Winston. I feared you were unwell."

Winston's chest puffed out at his fellow Stannum alumnus' concern. "No, no, I needed to do some work at the bank. You know how it is in business. Just because we are closed on Saturday, sometimes we need to go in to catch up on paperwork."

"Yes, successful business ventures require substantial attention." Turning to Jeanette, he continued, "As do other endeavors. I fear I am remiss in congratulating you on the engagement of your son. Did I hear you say he is to wed in December?"

Jeanette's face flushed. "I only wish it were something for which to be congratulated. I am sure you have heard some of the rumors about the girl, but John is determined to have her, and his grandmother supports him. I fear the girl's mother, Mrs. Stuart's secretary, wields significant influence over the household, and I am powerless to protect my poor son."

Vaughn rubbed his chin with one hand. "Yes, perhaps Mrs. Stuart has begun to lose some of her faculties. She was quite sharp at one time, but I have had some trouble even gaining an audience with her recently. Possibly you are correct about her secretary exercising an unnatural amount of influence. Mrs. Stuart must be nearing eighty, is she not?"

The important man's interest in her family made Jeanette sit up straighter. "Next year. I do hope she doesn't allow someone to fritter away substantial amounts of Stuart property and money. Winston and I offered once to assist her, but she refused. Quite rudely, too. I suspect that could also be a sign of a reduced mental capacity. She was always quite fond of me when I was married to Carlisle." She felt the blush under her makeup as she spoke the last and hoped no one could see it.

Vaughn bent close to speak so only Jeanette would hear. "Do not despair, Jeanette. Something may yet occur to improve the situation." He straightened and tugged on his wife's hand to lead her away.

~~~

Tuesday, October 11, 1955

When the boys burst through the front door after school, Sandra met them at the foot of the main staircase. "For a couple of young men who need to study for two tests tomorrow, you're in a jovial mood."

John bent for a quick kiss before they followed Matt into the parlor. "Well, one is in math, and you know Matt never needs to study for those. I think I have it down, too. We'll need to work on literature though. That's one of your specialties, so you can drill us after dinner."

"Yes, after my birthday dinner," Matt reminded them. "I hope Lila remembered everything I requested tonight."

Laughing, Sandra said, "I was in the kitchen when she made the hamburger patties. She grumbled the whole time."

"Good. I'd hate to disappoint her by choosing anything she enjoys preparing." Shifting topics slightly, he added, "Is Aunt Kate agreeable to us eating on the veranda? It isn't windy and won't be too cold if we eat before it gets dark."

"I don't know if she plans to join us there, but she said we could since it's your birthday wish. If she doesn't want to eat out there, I'm sure Mother will eat inside with her. Greg will enjoy sitting out there with us." She peeked at John from under her bangs. "I don't think your mother and Winston plan to join us tonight, John."

He turned his attention to the books he piled on the coffee table. "I wouldn't expect them to. Considering how tense things have been, it's for the best." His gaze flickered to Matt. "She still hasn't forgotten how vehemently Matt supported us when we started planning our wedding."

"Well, that's one birthday gift already," Matt said with a chuckle. He walked over and put his arm across his cousin's shoulders. "Sorry, John. I'm only kidding. I just hate how much of a damper she's put on what should be a happy time for you and Sandra."

After a moment, John nodded. "I know, and you're right." He turned and hugged the young man who was as close as a brother. "Thanks, Matt, and happy birthday. Let's go find Lila and Gramma Kate." He turned and held out an arm for Sandra, who slipped her hand through it. Matt offered her his arm also, and the three friends went in search of their benefactor and her longtime cook.

When they reached the kitchen, Matt stole up behind Lila, who was intent on decorating his birthday cake. When he leaned over her shoulder, she jumped and dragged the icing tip across the top of her masterpiece.

"Oh! Look what you made me do, you scamp," she exclaimed. "Now it's ruined."

To the amusement of John and Sandra, Matt kissed Lila's cheek as he snuck a finger around to steal some icing. "It's perfect, Lila, just like all your cakes. As soon as we can gobble down the delicious hamburgers you're making for me, we'll carve up the cake, and no one will remember you misspelled my name."

"I did not misspell it. You made me run it off the edge of the cake. Now get out of my kitchen and take your cohorts with you. And get your finger out of that icing. Did you think I didn't see that? I've known you too long. I know your tricks, Matt Hunter." She snatched up a dishtowel and swatted him with it.

"Ow, all right, I'm going." He pressed another kiss to her cheek, then danced out of range of the towel before she could strike again. "I hope you made enough burgers. John and I are hungry. I bet Jonah will be, too, when he gets here. We didn't see his truck when we came in, but I'm sure he'll have worked up a good appetite today."

"He told Mrs. Kathryn he finished the walls he's been working on and went into Elkford for something he needs for tomorrow. He said he'd be back in time for dinner."

"Good. With Jonah and Mary and Greg and Mrs. Duncan, that will make nine of us for dinner." He grinned at John. "So...two dozen burgers?"

Lila snorted. "If I make two dozen, you better eat every single one nobody else wants."

"We can reheat them tomorrow if there are any left."

"No, we won't. I don't serve reheated hamburgers."

"Lila, you don't serve burgers period if you can help it. You're only serving them tonight because Aunt Kate said I could choose whatever I wanted for my birthday dinner."

"Well, we finally found something we agree on." She put her hands on her hips and glared at him. "Now get on out of here while you're ahead."

Matt flashed one last grin. "Yes, ma'am." His hand darted out, and he raked a finger across the cake one more time before dodging the dishtowel. A laughing John and Sandra followed him out the kitchen door.

"Let's go look at the carriage house," John said. "If Jonah finished building the walls upstairs, we should be able to really get a feel for what it will look like once it's finished."

Sandra gripped John's arm. "It's wonderful. Mary and I walked over there after my lessons. It will be so cozy, John. I want to pick out paint for the kitchen and bathroom this weekend. Jonah said he would varnish the paneling in our bedroom and the baby's room next week. Then he can concentrate on the kitchen and bathroom cabinets. We need to pick light fixtures, too."

As the pair chattered about their future home, Matt trailed along behind them deep in thought. He had overheard a couple of Claudine's friends make further insulting comments about Sandra in the hall when he was on his way to English. Apparently, some of that group already forgot the message he sent via Rachel Pullen a few weeks earlier. He had been late for class, so he didn't take time to confront them, but he intended to hold a frank chat with them tomorrow. He would also make an example of someone again before the week ended and inform Aunt Kate when he could seize a few minutes alone with her. She would handle the gossips' mothers. He didn't plan to tell John or Sandra if he could avoid it. They had enough to deal with. Matt could handle the schoolgirls.

Chapter 13

Thursday, October 13, 1955

"Is that a real car?" Matt quipped.

John pulled to a halt beside the tiny vehicle and studied it a moment. "Yep, a Nash Metropolitan. Do you think it's Millie's new car?"

"Colonel Waters said he'd take her again today to look at cars after Sandra's lessons, didn't he?"

"Yes." After a few seconds of silence, John added, "The colonel's been great about taking her around to find something reliable she could afford. Pretty nice of him to take so much time to help out."

"Yep." Matt continued to stare at the petite car. "I like him. Do you?"

"Colonel Waters? Sure. He's been a good tutor for Sandra and helpful to her mom."

"Yep, real helpful. I think you better like him a lot. He might be around a long time."

John grinned at last. "Yeah, I thought that, too. If Millie likes him and Sandra likes him, he's OK with me."

"Come on, let's go find out about this minicar." Matt pushed open his door and scooped up his books.

They found Sandra in the parlor studying. "Hey, honey," John greeted her. He leaned down to kiss her, then asked, "Is that your mom's new car outside?"

"Yes." She giggled at the expression on Matt's face. "Isn't it cute? They say it can hold four people, but two would need to be tiny to fit in the back. It will be fine for her and Greg though."

"We should have brought him home with us instead of dropping him at your mom's house. He'll be thrilled with it," Matt said.

"I expect there will be teasing involved when his friends see it. I'm at a good spot to take a break from reading this story. Let's go find Mother and Colonel Waters. They're going through the owner's manual. He wants her to know how to work everything."

When the three teens reached the great room, Kathryn beckoned to John to follow her to the study, leaving Matt and Sandra with Millie and the colonel.

Once John closed the door, Kathryn gestured for him to join her in the leather chairs in front of the glowing coal fire in the small fireplace. "Your mother called this morning. She is on another rampage about you and Sandra marrying. She also tried to order me to send you to her cottage to live full-time. I refused, of course."

John slumped into the chair beside his grandmother. "Did something happen to set her off?"

"She claims she had to learn from Reverend Walker that you and Sandra set a wedding date. That's untrue, of course. You told her when you stopped to pick up more of your winter clothing weeks ago, did you not?"

"Yes, ma'am, but she wasn't interested in listening. I told her we were to marry at noon on December twenty-third at the church, but she was talking over me about how Sandra was lying about being pregnant and if she wasn't that the baby couldn't possibly be mine. I'm afraid I quit trying to give her details about the wedding after that, but I did tell her the time and date and place. If she chose to ignore me, there's nothing I can do about it. She's irrational about Sandra and the baby."

He leaned forward, propping his head in his hands before he continued. "I'm afraid that's going to continue for a long time. I don't know whether to hope she will show up for the wedding or not. She might try to disrupt it, and I don't want that to be the memory Sandra or I have of our wedding, Gramma."

Kathryn reached across and placed a hand on his arm. "I shall not allow that to happen, John. For your sake, I hope she sees reason. While she and I do not hold one another in high regard, she is still your mother and should attend. However, she shall attend in support of you, or at the least remain silent during the service and reception."

"I hope she will, Gramma. I hate this situation. A part of me would like to take Sandra and elope."

"Nonsense. You would miss having your family with you at such an important time and so would Sandra. You're both close to what little family you have. Let me handle your mother. I didn't mean to burden you with her latest antics, but I thought it best I made you aware."

"Yes," John sighed. "I need to know in case she pulls something when you aren't around."

~~~

Friday, October 14, 1955

Matt had delivered his warning on Wednesday. He even let them know he would make an example of somebody soon to ensure they knew he was serious about them not making up and spreading tales about Sandra. It took him two more days to plan and execute his scheme. He had used the Stuart library to fine tune the instrument of his attack. It would cost him a few points on his grade, but the price another would pay would be much dearer.

He entered his American history class and chose a seat in the center aisle almost to the back of the room. He shifted it forward a few inches to ensure it sat slightly ahead of the flanking seats. He was one of the first to arrive, and he hoped Jillian stayed true to form. Despite the vehemence he directed at her and Claudine's other friends, she still made a point to sit near him when they shared a class.

When she entered and chose the seat to his left, he allowed himself a smile. Now to get just the right question to execute his plan. He had something prepared for three different possibilities. He just needed one to be on the exam. Mrs. Thompkins passed out the test papers, part multiple choice and part short essay as promised. Matt flipped to the ten essay questions first and scanned through them. There was one of his targets at the top of the third page. Perfect.

He flipped back to the front and took care of the first section, careful to keep his left arm across the desk to block prying eyes from his multiple-choice answers. While John was a better student in history, Matt was no slouch. He should make an "A" on the test under normal circumstances, though today would likely not be one of those.

When he reached the question about the Battle of New Orleans during the War of 1812, he wrote out one of the carefully worded answers he crafted and memorized earlier. Once he finished writing the three lines required, he set aside his pencil and took a minute to stretch, relieving a twinge in his shoulder. Satisfied he had accomplished his goal, he picked up his pencil and shifted his left arm into blocking position again. Ten minutes later, he had completed the test and checked his answers.

The class ended, and he dropped his paper onto the pile on Mrs. Thompkins' desk with a huge grin. "Great test, Mrs. Thompkins. I've never enjoyed taking a history test as much as this one. Have a nice weekend."

~~~

When Matt left his last class of the day, he happened to pass Mrs. Thompkins' door. She stood waiting. "Mr. Hunter, please come in here for a moment."

He did as instructed and took a seat in the front row when she pointed to it. "Is something wrong, Mrs. Thompkins?" He couldn't keep the grin off his face.

"Since when did Hannibal Barca fight in the Battle of New Orleans, leading a battalion of Hessians in support of Andrew Jackson, no less?"

"Is that incorrect? I could have sworn we discussed those details in class earlier this week."

"Apparently your memory is shared by another classmate. One who happened to sit quite near you during today's test. Amazingly, that student gave almost a verbatim answer to that question. Based on that student's orientation to your seat, I'm sure you could not have done the copying. Therefore, I must assume you were the victim here, and we both know you were aware an attempt would be made to copy your answer."

"I assure you I did not copy someone else's answer, Mrs. Thompkins. Was my incorrect answer to the Battle of New Orleans question the only one you suspect was copied?"

"It appears so. You and I both know you carefully created that answer to entrap someone for cheating. I suspect specifically the person who copied it. Would you like to say anything further before I take this matter to the principal?"

"No, Mrs. Thompkins, though I have one question."

She pinched the bridge of her nose as she shook her head. "No, as far as I know it is not against the rules to write out an outrageously incorrect answer to prove someone cheated off your paper. That was your question, wasn't it?"

"Yes, ma'am. I didn't think it was, but I wasn't positive."

"You were willing to take your punishment if necessary? It was that important to trap this person?"

"Yes, Mrs. Thompkins, more than you can imagine."

"Well, you succeeded. There is no way she or her parents can argue she gave such a similarly incorrect answer."

"Good." He checked his watch. "I need to get to the cross-country team meeting if you don't have anything further, Mrs. Thompkins."

Shaking her head, she said, "No, that's all I wanted to discuss with you. Now I need to go talk to the principal. Good luck with your meet tomorrow, Matt."

"Thank you, Mrs. Thompkins." He popped up and sauntered out of the classroom. It had been a very good day for Matt Hunter.

~~~

Saturday, October 15, 1955

"There's hardly anybody at their meets, and it's the only one in Elkford each year," Sandra rationalized. She nibbled on her lip as she considered the repercussions. She had remained clear of the high school on her rare forays into Elkford in the last several weeks. However, John wanted to attend the cross-country meet to support Matt. So did Sandra. "We can watch along a part of the course away from the start and finish?"

Placing an encouraging arm around her, John said, "Yes, we can cut across our pasture and park along the fence line. They'll run right by us and we'll still be on Gramma's property where the park touches it. Matt knows to expect me there cheering him on. Greg wants to go, so I told him I'd pick him up on the way. Asa is running, too, and I told Greg to invite Caleb to meet us there so he can watch with us if he wants."

"All right, I'll go with you. Let me change into slacks since we'll be trudging around the pasture. When it's over, we can go pick out the kitchen and bathroom paint."

Forty-five minutes later, John, Sandra, and Greg pulled up to the entrance to the Stuart's lowest pasture. Greg hopped out and swung open the gate.

"Just leave it open, Greg," John called. "We don't have any cattle down here right now, so it's safe."

Greg jumped back in the car, and John drove forward across the field, careful to go slow and avoid any rocks or holes lurking under the grass. He reached the best vantage point along the fence dividing the pasture from the adjacent city park and stopped with the car parallel to the fence to allow them to sit on the hood and trunk to watch.

A lanky youth appeared in the distance walking in their direction, and Greg waved. "There's Caleb." The boy reached the fence and climbed up to join his friend atop a fencepost.

They heard the pop of the starter's gun in the distance. Occasionally, they could catch a glimpse of runners on the far side of the park through the trees. Sandra was busy trying to identify Matt when she heard a car approaching behind them. Her stomach lurched. Would someone trespass on the Stuart's property to confront her about trapping John? Then she recognized Perry's car. Crammed into it were Maria and several of their loyal friends, few of whom Sandra had seen during her seclusion at Chestnut Cove or on her rare trips into Elkford.

After several minutes of teary, enthusiastic greetings, Greg called, "Hey, you're going to miss the main event over here."

The friends moved back around to the fence just in time for the lead runners to come into view. Matt strode along at the rear of the first pack. He waved when his friends broke into cheers. Asa followed in the next group, receiving another round of support as he passed.

"How long until they make the next lap?" Maria asked.

"Ten or fifteen minutes," John replied.

"Good, that gives us time to fill you in on what I heard last night at the game." She gestured for the group to huddle closer. "Mrs. Thompkins had Jillian called to the principal's office after school. They called her parents and told them they had to come to the school. She got caught cheating on our history test yesterday. Apparently, she copied somebody's answer almost exactly."

"How did they know who copied whom?" Sandra asked.

"Partly from where the two students were seated, but also because the student she copied from practically told Mrs. Thompkins something was up. The answer Jillian copied was wrong–really wrong. Somebody made up a wild answer to draw Mrs. Tompkins' attention when she graded it and ensure she remembered when she saw the same one later."

"What happened to Jillian? What did the principal do?"

"She's been suspended. They would have put her in detention and given her a zero on the test, but she argued and lied so much that the principal had enough and suspended her for two weeks. She can't even attend games or anything. I bet she doesn't graduate. Her grades are bad already. I don't know how she can pass now."

"Gosh, that's terrible," Sandra said. "I miss being at school. I know she will, too. I feel sorry for her."

Maria hugged her friend. "Sandra, you are a sweetheart. You know Jillian is one of the girls who has said terrible things about you. It might be mean to say, but she's getting what she deserves for being so awful."

"Hey," Greg called. "Here comes another couple of Elkford's runners."

The group returned their attention to the race. John lifted Sandra up onto the hood of his car so she could see better. Before he could turn around to watch, she leaned down to whisper in his ear. "Did you know anything about it?"

"About Jillian getting suspended? No, I'd have told you. Must have happened after I left school."

"No, about Matt's plot. You and I both know this has his name written all over it."

John cleared his throat and stole a look at the others. "No, he knows better than to tell me about any chicanery. I bet Gramma knows though. They're too much alike."

At last, Sandra giggled. "Yes, they are. McDougals through and through."

Chapter 14

Saturday, November 5, 1955

Sandra smoothed her hands down the front of her new dress. She had abandoned all her old clothes over the last month as the bulge of her abdomen began to grow. Almost two weeks ago, she felt the first flutter of the baby moving. She and John had been alone in the parlor studying. When she realized it felt just the way her mother and the new obstetrician described, she grabbed John's hand and held it to her belly. He hadn't been able to feel anything, but his excitement wasn't the less for it. She had felt it, and he was ecstatic.

Jonah had their carriage house apartment finished. She and John and Matt had joined Jonah upstairs Thursday evening to measure and discuss placement of furniture. They would need to buy a couple of pieces–notably the sofa Matt wanted to be able to sleep on–but most of what they would use was the old furniture John and Jonah moved downstairs earlier. A few pieces would be refinished, something Jonah would do for them also. Others only required cleaning before they could be moved back into the apartment.

The primary things needed besides the sofa were a new mattress for their antique iron bed and furniture for the baby's room. Sandra and Millie had looked at baby beds and highchairs and playpens, but Sandra wanted John to see and approve everything before she bought them. An old wardrobe would serve the needs of storing the baby's clothes, diapers, and toys when Jonah redid it.

"Sandra?" John called. "Are you upstairs?"

"Yes, in my room." She heard him on the stairs, and then his head rounded the corner of her open door.

"Jonah's here to help us move the furniture. You said you wanted to be there when we start taking it up."

She glowed in excitement. "Yes, I do." She grabbed his hand and dragged him back toward the stairs. "Hasn't it been the greatest week? The apartment is finished and we completed our counseling sessions with Reverend Walker last Sunday evening and I got another good report from Colonel Waters on my schoolwork and I can feel the baby moving more and now we're going to move the first of our furniture into the apartment!"

They reached the foyer landing, and John pulled her into his arms and kissed her for a full minute. When they broke apart, he whispered, "It's been a great week, and things will only get better over the next few months. We get married in just under seven weeks. We'll have everything perfect in the apartment by then, and we'll get to move in and wake up together on Christmas Eve and Christmas morning and all the mornings after that."

When they finally exited the house, they found Matt and Jonah lounging on the tailgate of Jonah's truck. "About time you two got out here," Matt taunted around a piece of hay he was chewing. "I get a Saturday off from running before districts next weekend, and you two leave me to sit here waiting for you to start moving your furniture into your apartment. I say we go on strike, Jonah. What do you think?"

"Suits me. It's not like they don't have more work I need to do on their furniture. I could be sanding that table getting it ready to varnish instead of hanging out here waiting on those two to quit smooching. You know that's what they were doing, right Matt?"

"Oh yeah, they do that a lot when they think nobody will notice."

Laughing, John said, "Enough. Let's get what doesn't need any work done to it cleaned up and moved."

An hour later, the four sat around what would serve as their dining room table. Gaps remained in the furnishings, but it was close enough for Sandra and John to envision living there soon.

"Why don't we go into town and look at sofas and buy your mattress?" Matt suggested.

John clapped his hand on Matt's shoulder. "Afraid we'll renege on the sofa promise?"

"Yes. I want to test it out before you buy it, too. I want it nice and comfy in case Aunt Kate gets extra mad at me and I need it for several nights."

Jonah dug his keys out of his pocket and tossed them to John. "Take my truck. I won't need it this afternoon. I have everything I need to work on the furniture that needs refinishing. If you find a sofa or mattress you want, you can bring it back on my truck instead of waiting for them to deliver it sometime next week."

John passed his car keys to Jonah. "Thanks, Jonah. Take these in case something comes up and you need wheels while we're gone."

When the truck returned later, Matt climbed out beaming. A long sofa sat strapped in the back with a mattress standing on edge beside it.

Jonah wandered out of the lower level of the carriage house where he was sanding. Tilting his head one way and then the other, he pointed at Matt. "You're going to carry that monster up with John, not me." He retreated to his work, shaking his head as he went.

~~~

Monday, November 7, 1955

A knock caused Reverend Walker to jump. Intent on researching a passage to quote for his sermon, he hadn't heard any other sound to alert him to the presence of the woman who stood in his office doorway.

"Hello, may I help you?" He didn't recognize her. Certainly not a member of his congregation. Perhaps in her mid-twenties, she wore a conservative gray skirt and jacket with black heels. She reminded him of his older daughter who married and moved to Woodbury a year earlier.

Her whole body seemed to tremble, and she took a quick look over her shoulder. "I'm sorry to bother you, Reverend, but...well, I felt the need to talk to someone, and I saw a car in the church parking lot and found the outer door unlocked." She stopped, as if unsure how much more to explain without an invitation to remain.

Walker stood and held out a hand. "Please, come in and be seated. I stayed late to do some work this evening. I'll be happy to sit and listen if you need someone to talk to. I'm Reverend Walker."

The woman took a few tentative steps into the room and shook hands with the pastor before settling herself on the edge of a chair. "Thank you, Reverend Walker. I'm new in Elkford and have no one to..." A sob shook her, and she dug a handkerchief from her purse to dab at her eyes. "I'm sorry. It's just been so hard."

Returning to his seat, Walker said, "Our congregation would welcome you joining us. Why don't you tell me something about yourself, your family, why you came to Elkford, Miss...?"

"Dixon," she replied. "Althea Dixon. I'd like that." She sniffled, wiped her nose, and seemed to relax. "I moved here a few weeks ago. Actually, I came to Woodbury to take a job first, but it fell through at the last minute. I couldn't find anything else there right away, so I came to Elkford. I'm a trained secretary, but there don't seem to be any such jobs open here either. The town is lovely, and I would so like to remain here, but I must find a job. I'm down to my last five dollars." She broke into sobs again and buried her face in her hands.

The pastor took out a key and unlocked a drawer. Pulling out a metal box, he opened it and took out two ten-dollar bills. He made a note on a slip of paper before rising to circle his desk. "Miss Dixon, the church maintains a small fund for emergencies. It isn't much, but I can give you twenty dollars to help you out financially. You are also welcome to dine with my family this evening. My wife will be pleased to add another place at the table." He leaned against the front of his desk and held out the two bills to her.

Althea turned her tear-streaked face upward. "Oh, Reverend Walker, that is unbelievably kind of you." One arm reached toward the money, but suddenly she snatched the bills and lurched out of her chair toward him. Her arms snaked around his shoulders, her body pressing him against the desk, and her lips smashed into his, smearing red lipstick across his face.

His hands reached up for her arms to push her away as a flash of light and telltale poof sounded from the doorway. Before he could react, another followed. He gripped the girl's arms and twisted them away from his neck before pushing her back.

"Thanks, Rev," said the man holding the camera. "Come on, doll." The grinning woman gave a wave to the pastor, the tens fluttering in her hand, before following the photographer out of the office.

~~~

Wednesday, November 9, 1955

"I can't believe we're getting married six weeks from Friday." Sandra fingered the stiff petticoat hung in the guest bedroom being used for wedding preparations. That the room formerly belonged to John's parents–and to Jeanette from the time of her first husband's death until her remarriage–remained an unspoken incongruity among the family and staff at Chestnut Cove. "Are you sure we can fit my dress properly so I can get into it and breathe in six more weeks? How much bigger will my stomach get by then?"

Millie held up the bodice, already tacked together. "Yes, that's why we chose an empire waist for it. We'll allow plenty of room for you to grow when we make the skirt, and it will have enough fullness and pleats that you won't show too much." She beckoned for her daughter to return to the low stool in the center of the room. "Up here. Lila and I need to measure."

Sandra did as instructed, turning and moving her arms while Millie and Lila held up the material and pinned and marked and discussed and repeated the process. "Did Cindy's letter say when she would get here for Christmas?"

Mumbling around the pins in the left corner of her mouth, Millie replied, "No, but she said if Calvin can't get leave in time for them to arrive at least two days before the wedding, she'll come ahead of him. She can take the train and let him drive when he can get away."

"At least they can come this year. I missed her when they were posted so far away. I'm glad the army moved him back to this side of the country." Lila carefully removed the material from around Sandra and allowed her to step down. "Whew, I'm tired, and all I did was stand up there while y'all fitted. Did Cindy send her measurements? Is she close enough to Mary like you thought that Mary can play pincushion for you on Cindy's dress until the final fitting?"

"Yes, Mary should work fine for a mannequin."

The girl giggled from her seat in the corner. "I get double duty, first getting Cindy's dress fitted and then my dress for serving and seeing to the bride's book. Speaking of the book, have you picked one out yet?" Mary hopped up when her mother pointed from her to the stool Sandra just abandoned.

"Yes," Sandra replied. She took Mary's chair. "We ordered one when we were at the stationery store yesterday. John is to pick it up tomorrow after school." She hopped back up and grabbed a notepad from the dresser. "We picked out invitations, too, but we didn't order them yet. We need to finalize the guest list to know how many to order." She began to scan the names of invitees. After their outing at the cross-country meet, she and John decided to add their friends they had been concerned about putting into a bad position earlier. They didn't want to cause trouble between any of their friends and their parents, but those closest had assured the couple that there would be no repercussions for attending the wedding. "With family and friends, we're up to almost fifty."

From the doorway, Kathryn asked, "Are you including the parents of your friends? You need to add them if you have not done so. They may not choose to attend, but if they are willing to allow their children to do so, then they should be afforded an invitation also."

"Yes, Grandmother Kathryn. We thought about that and intended to ask your opinion and Mother's. We'll add them." Sandra started through the list, penciling in the additional names next to their children's.

"I suggest we place the invitation order no later than Friday. Order a dozen or more above what you expect to need in case you realize someone has been left off. It is best to have extras."

"Yes, ma'am. We have the time, date, place, and all those details set, and we already told the stationery store what style and color we want. All we need to do is call them with the number we need. I'll let John and you and Mother look at the list one last time before we count the number of invitations." She went back to the top of her list and began to check the names again.

Chapter 15

Thursday, November 17, 1955

"Let me see if she's available, Reverend Walker." Millie pressed the receiver to her palm while she waited for her employer to indicate if she would speak to the pastor right then.

Kathryn held out her hand, and Millie passed the telephone across. "Good morning, Reverend. To what do I owe such an early call?" The elderly woman's brows contracted almost immediately. As she waited without comment for him to finish, her eyes narrowed to slits.

At last, she said, "I see. That is most displeasing, Mr. Walker. I cannot account for why you would come to such a decision at this point in time. We discussed the issue in detail weeks ago, and you acceded to our request. The couple completed their six counseling sessions with you more than a week ago."

Millie sat in the chair she normally used for taking dictation and discussing schedules and other details with Mrs. Stuart and listened to the one-sided conversation. Her eyes darted to the wall separating the study from the parlor where Sandra and her tutor worked. When Kathryn hung up the phone after several terse comments, Millie already knew the gist of what would be said next.

"We must settle upon a new venue and a new minister for the wedding. Mr. Walker has rescinded his decision to both preside over the event and to allow it to occur at the church."

Rubbing her eyes, Millie asked, "Did he give any reason for his sudden change of mind? Does he realize what a position he has put us in? The wedding is only five weeks away."

"He apologized, but he said the matter had weighed on his conscience and he came to this decision last night." Kathryn tapped a pencil on the desk. "Something in the tone of his voice gives me pause." She stared into space for several seconds, and Millie sat quietly waiting. When the older woman took a deep breath and shifted her attention to the secretary, she said, "I believe something more is at work here. I will go into Elkford this afternoon and speak to Reverend Walker in person. In the meantime, we must consider our options."

"If it's all right with you, Mrs. Stuart, I would rather not tell Sandra until we know more about what happened and have an alternative to suggest. She's ahead of schedule with her coursework, and I would like for her to finish the first semester lessons before Thanksgiving. Colonel Waters believes she can complete all her senior coursework before the baby arrives at her current pace. Fretting about the wedding being turned upside down might upset her enough to delay that."

"Yes, of course. I agree that there is no reason to bother her or John until we know more and I have an opportunity to speak to the reverend in person and attempt to persuade him to change his mind." Kathryn picked up her calendar and scanned it. "I wonder at the timing, also." She made a notation and flipped over to December.

"Millie," the matriarch continued, "would you dial the church in Inverness for me? The number is in my address book. We attended it years ago, and it is slightly closer than the one in Elkford. However, we chose to move our membership to Elkford once Alistair's business expanded there. I retain many friendships in Inverness and would be pleased to return to that church should we not come to terms with Reverend Walker."

"You believe they would agree to host the wedding on short notice?"

"Yes, I do. I would tend to err in that direction now. I would not want to change Mr. Walker's mind this afternoon only for him to change it again even closer to the wedding."

"Yes, Ma'am, that occurred to me, also."

~~~

When he heard a knock on his door, Reverend Walker's heart jerked. Wild eyes darted around, expecting to see yet another unwelcome visitor. The woman standing behind his secretary wasn't likely to cause the same torment he suffered over the last ten days, but it would be equally painful.

"Mrs. Stuart, I didn't expect to see you. I'm sorry, but I must leave for an appointment momentarily." He saw the confusion in his secretary's eyes. "I'm sorry, I forgot to tell you, Mrs. Hill." He stood and began gathering a hodgepodge of things to take with him.

Kathryn Stuart stepped around the woman and pushed the door closed. "I shall not take more than a couple of minutes of your time. I only want you to look me in the eye and tell me you are refusing to marry my grandson and his fiancée in this church as we agreed. I also want you to give me your real reason, not the mishmash you spouted on the telephone."

The pastor looked everywhere except at the church's largest patron. "I'm sorry, Mrs. Stuart. I simply must go now. I apologize for the change in my position, but after much thought over the last two weeks, I realized I made an error in consenting to conduct the wedding." He grabbed up his briefcase and raked a pile of papers into it. Several missed and spilled onto his chair and the floor. He bent to collect them and banged his head on the desk.

"You have been the minister at this church for some years now. I have been most pleased with you until today. I have never known you to lie, Reverend, but you are lying to me now. Moreover, you are lying to yourself. I want to know why you changed your mind about this wedding." The last words echoed around the office and found their mark.

He slumped into his chair and held his head in his hands. "I can't, Mrs. Stuart. I'm sorry, but I can't. I have no choice in the matter."

Kathryn settled herself in one of the chairs opposite him, coincidentally the same one the girl sat in for her brief visit ten days prior. "Someone forced you to make this decision. They have something to hold over you?"

He nodded without looking up. "They set me up. I would never do such a thing, but they made it look like I had and took photographs." He opened his desk drawer and took out a manila envelope. Holding it upside down over his desk, he shook it until two pictures and a typed note fell out. "This girl came to my office late one afternoon after Mrs. Hill left early last week. She was upset and needed someone to talk to and some financial help, or so she said. When she saw an opportunity, she sprang at me and kissed me." Wild eyes looked at Kathryn, begging her to believe him. "I swear I did nothing to encourage her. I love my wife and have always been a faithful husband. I try hard to live by the words I preach."

She frowned at the distasteful scene in the two snapshots, the girl with her arms wrapped around the pastor. "You realize the fact whoever is behind this had a photographer ready to take those..." She pointed at the desk. "It virtually proves you were set up."

"For many people, yes, but some will claim this is a habit in which I indulge, and someone merely sought to prove it. I cannot risk my career or my marriage, Mrs. Stuart. I must be able to feed and house my family. Whoever did this threatens to ensure that the next time will leave no doubt of my perfidy."

"I see. The price for withholding these photos from the public is to refuse to marry my grandson?"

"Yes, Mrs. Stuart. I'm sorry."

She reached across and picked up the note. After examining it in detail, she placed it back on his desk, stood, and walked to the door. "I am sorry, too, Mr. Walker. Most sorry. I fear by not making this matter public you will remain beholden to this scoundrel forever."

~~~

When Kathryn returned to Chestnut Cove, she went straight to the study and closed the door, leaving her secretary along with the young members of her household to wonder at the unusual action. She emerged two hours later and went to the parlor where John, Sandra, and Matt sat doing homework.

"Matt, can you leave your schoolwork to attend me in the study for a few minutes?" He rose in silence and followed her.

As soon as he closed the door behind them, she said, "Reverend Walker is being blackmailed. Someone staged a scene involving a young woman and had a photographer on hand to capture it. He received an anonymous note along with copies of the photographs. The note instructs him to refuse to hold John and Sandra's wedding at the church or conduct the ceremony himself at any other location. I have no choice but to inform John and Sandra of the sordid details because I will not have them think they are responsible. However, I wished to inform you first and to ask you to maintain an awareness of anything which might indicate the perpetrator."

Matt sat and leaned forward, placing his elbows on his knees and his chin on his hands. "Do you think Jeanette or Winston is behind this? I think it sounds too well-thought-out and executed for them."

Kathryn smiled at his perception. "I agree. While Jeanette spouts her vitriol readily and tries to cajole John and others to obey her wishes, she universally fails at the latter and is not known to otherwise act on the former. No, I believe someone else instigated this, and there are few people in Elkford with the ability, resources, and viciousness to accomplish it."

Raising his eyes to meet his aunt's, Matt said, "Someone has a serious axe to grind. Not over a wedding between two teenagers. This is aimed at you, not John and Sandra."

She nodded. "I believe that to be the case."

"That man at the country club who's been harassing you to sell it...he also tried to get you to sell him a building in Elkford a couple of years ago and you refused?"

"Yes, Vaughn Michaelson. I have watched him for some time now. He is someone who craves power and respect and money and has proven ruthless in some business dealings. I understand he has a voracious appetite for many things. His father died unexpectedly several years ago, leaving the son a small but profitable liquor distribution business." She stopped and waited to ensure she had Matt's complete attention. "His first wife died about a year ago. He recently married again to a young lady from a wealthy family in Woodbury, raising his social status further. He was also a schoolmate of Winston Hathaway's at Stannum Academy, though I believe he was two or three grades behind."

"So he is likely to have heard Jeanette ranting her nonsense about Sandra trapping John into marrying her. He might intend to do a favor for Jeanette and Winston, requested or not, by interfering with the wedding plans."

"That is my hypothesis. I have little proof to support it, but I have been able to think of no alternative that makes sense. I also have no power to correct the matter with Reverend Walker. However, I have already placed a call to arrange an appointment for another wedding venue. I have contacted the church in Inverness and arranged to visit it tomorrow."

"That's a great idea, Aunt Kate. You intend for us to move our membership back there, I assume."

"I do. If you will summon the others, I will inform them of this matter and my plans to remedy the situation. First, I wanted to give you the facts and allow you to assess them and learn if your conclusion would match my own. For now, keep your eyes and ears open, Matt. I fear that man will be an issue long after I depart this life."

Matt pressed his lips together and nodded. "Yes, Aunt Kate. I will." He rose and went in search of Millie, John, and Sandra.

~~~

Friday, November 18, 1955

"Five weeks! I can't believe we're changing the location of our wedding now. We haven't even picked up the invitations and now they're wrong! What if they refuse to let us marry here, too? What if somebody blackmails this pastor?" Sandra slept little the previous night. The calm which had descended on events over the last few weeks shattered with the news they couldn't marry in the church they attended. Kathryn had assured the girl things should go smoothly today, though she didn't share the rationale for such optimism with anyone.

Millie squeezed her daughter's hand, trying to settle her nerves. "It will all work out, dear. Mrs. Stuart has a long connection with this church. Remember, this is where her husband and John's father are buried. The Stuarts attended here for years before they moved their membership into Elkford. Do you remember attending John's father's funeral here?"

"Yes, I remember. We drive out here sometimes to put flowers on his grave. John likes to come and sit on the bench at the foot of his grandfather's grave and be quiet and remember them." She wiped at her eyes with a handkerchief. "I'm sorry to be so fussy. I appreciate everyone trying to work this out for us."

Vance, who had offered to drive the ladies after he and Sandra finished her lessons, sat quietly in the front seat listening. He stole a look at the matriarch, seated beside him in the front seat. "Your family attended the church in Inverness for quite some time, Mrs. Stuart?" Vance asked.

"Yes, Inverness is closer, but it is little more than a crossroads. Alistair and I thought it prudent to move our membership to the church in Elkford as his business dealings expanded. He spent most of his time there, dealt with bankers and transport companies and so forth there. However, we maintained ties to the smaller church in Inverness. When our elder son died in the Great War, we brought him home to be buried there alongside Alistair's parents in the Stuart lot. Of course, Alistair and Carlisle joined them in recent years. My own McDougal family also has a lot in the cemetery. I had considered in the years since Alistair's death returning my membership to Inverness. Now I regret not doing so sooner." She fell silent, and Vance didn't press for further information.

When they pulled into the gravel parking area of the church, a woman hurried out of a building attached to the side of the sanctuary. She went straight to the front passenger door and hugged the Stuart matriarch as soon as she stepped from her car.

"Hello, Gwen. I appreciate you meeting us this morning," Kathryn said.

"Nonsense. I've waited for years for you to return to us. The Reverend is inside working on his sermon. He'll join us in the sanctuary. I have the papers for you. We can handle the rest of the family Sunday."

"That will be perfect. Here, allow me to introduce everyone." She held out her hand to Sandra, and the girl stepped to the elderly woman's side. "This is Sandra Duncan, John's fiancée. Sandra, this is Gwen McPherson. Her elder sister was one of my dearest friends. She's gone now, but Gwen and I have been friends also for nearly seventy years." She continued, pointing to Millie and Vance in turn. "This is Sandra's mother, and my indispensable secretary, Millie Duncan, and that is Colonel Waters. He is Sandra's tutor and has become a good friend to us, also."

"Oh, it's so nice to meet all of you. Come, come. Let's go in. You can look around the sanctuary and sort out details away from this wind." The group exchanged greetings and then followed her into the church.

Once inside, Millie walked to the front to consider possible flower placement, spacing of the wedding party, and overall size of the room compared to the previous venue. Vance accompanied her, giving his opinion when requested. Sandra took the opportunity to confront her primary concern with Gwen and Kathryn. "I don't mean to seem ungrateful or petulant, but Mrs. Stuart said she told you what happened with the other pastor. How can you be sure something won't cause this one to change his mind at the last minute like the one in Elkford? I can't..." She felt the tears beginning to pool in her eyes and stopped before her voice could crack.

"Oh dear, no." Gwen wrapped her arms around the girl. "Such a terrible thing for them to do to you and John. I assure you that won't happen here. No, we will be thrilled for you to marry in our church. Ralph is quite pleased about it."

"Ralph?" Sandra didn't remember anyone named Ralph being mentioned.

"Reverend McPherson, my husband. Ralph and I have been all around the state since he was ordained more than forty years ago. We finally got to come home for him to finish his career as a minister right here where we both grew up. I assure you he won't back out of holding your wedding. I wouldn't let him hear the end of it if he tried, though he would never do such a thing. He would certainly never be intimidated by any staged photographs of him with some hussy or any other stunt someone might pull."

The tears spilled down Sandra's cheeks, and she squeezed Gwen tightly. "Oh, thank you. Thank you so very much."

Chapter 16

Matt burst through the front door. "We're here," he proclaimed. Earl Hunter trailed his son at a slower pace, but he wore the same broad smile. "I'll take your suitcase up, Dad. Go ahead downstairs. Aunt Kate and John and Sandra should be there." The teen bounded up toward the third-floor room his father would occupy for the holidays, and Earl walked down the familiar half flight of steps to the main hall of the mansion.

Kathryn appeared from the smaller hallway to the study. "Hello, Earl, it's good to have you here again for a few days. How was your trip?"

"Fine, Mrs. Kathryn." He took her outstretched hand and kissed her cheek. "I still hate we needed to reduce our passenger runs through Woodbury and cut out those on the Elkford line entirely. Otherwise I'd have arrived earlier. However, you and I are both aware times are changing. Too many people driving themselves across the region now."

"Indeed, I fear the railroad may cut out even freight to Elkford in another ten years. Our own demand for transport is down, and I gather we are not alone." She gestured for him to precede her into the great room. "John and Sandra are in here." Clomping on the stairs signaled Matt's return also. "Commerce is an ever-evolving thing. I've discussed that with John on several occasions. The demand for products his grandfather manufactured in great quantity during the war went down afterward, and we shifted to other things. We must do our best to predict the market even as we fulfill current demand. The same is true for you at the railroad."

"Hello, Uncle Earl," John said when Earl and Kathryn entered the great room. "As usual, you and Gramma couldn't wait for you to get into the house good before you began to discuss business."

Earl extended his hand, and the two shook. "Why should this visit be any different? How are you, John?"

"Fine. You remember Sandra?"

"Yes, of course. Hello, dear. I'm pleased you're to join the family soon. I look forward to attending your wedding in a few weeks. I understand there was a last-minute hitch, but it's been sorted out now."

Sandra shook hands with him. "Yes, it has. We attended services at the church in Inverness Sunday. It's a beautiful country church. I'm happy we're getting married there."

"You and John will be joining a long line of family members who married there, including myself and Eleanor."

"So I've learned, Mr. Hunter. I knew Matt's mother and grandparents and John's father and grandfather and others were buried there, but I had no idea about the long association with it until the last several days. Grandmother Kathryn told me about it, and I would love to hear your stories sometime also if you wouldn't mind."

"I would love to, Sandra."

"Before anybody gets caught up in telling tales, dinner is about to be on the table, or it will be if I can get some help in here." Lila stood in the dining room doorway pointing a spoon at the three young people.

"Hello, Lila," Earl said with a grin. "Why don't we all come help carry things for you?"

"Hey, Mr. Earl. Good to see you. Nice to have some volunteer help for once. Mary's down with Jonah's family tonight, so I'm long on folks to feed and short on help."

Earl scowled at his son. "I hope she's teasing about not getting help. Come on, Matt, let's get dinner served."

"I help so much I could get a job as a maître d', Dad," Matt replied. As soon as they entered the kitchen, he placed a dishtowel over his arm and bowed. "See? Got it down to a science. I can do housecleaning, too. I change my sheets and sweep and dust in my room. I even used the vacuum one day. Wish I had a patent on that thing."

A parade of the male occupants and guests carried the various dishes into the dining room and placed them on the table. Sandra and Lila followed with the last of the food, and soon the older members of the group were telling stories from days past.

When the phone rang toward the end of dessert, Lila rose to answer it, but Kathryn waved her off and stood. "I'll get it. You finish telling your story." She slipped behind John and Sandra and walked into the great room to the phone beside her chair. "Stuart residence," she answered. A choked-off reply was followed by silence. "Hello?"

Finally, a voice Kathryn knew well spoke. "Good evening, Mrs. Stuart. I hardly expected you to answer the phone yourself."

"Ah, good evening, Mrs. Hathaway. I'm sorry if my doing so somehow perplexed you. To what do I owe the honor of your call this evening?"

"I simply wished to inform John that we have reservations for dinner tomorrow at the club at two o'clock. I prefer he come to the house first so the three of us may ride there together."

Kathryn eased down into her chair. "I am afraid your invitation is both rather late and incomplete, Mrs. Hathaway. Surely you do not expect John to eat Thanksgiving dinner anywhere without his fiancée. Also, he already has plans to dine here tomorrow with the rest of his family. If you wished to offer him an alternative, surely good breeding requires you to issue such an invitation much earlier."

"He is my son. I should not be required to issue an invitation to him to eat Thanksgiving dinner with me."

"He no longer resides under your roof. You refuse to accept his soon-to-be bride. You have repeatedly denigrated her and his child she carries. What would possibly give you reason to expect him to spend a family holiday with you should you have issued a reasonably-timed invitation, much less without one? I suggest you invite him and his fiancée to visit you some other time in the near future if you can maintain a pleasant demeanor and remain cordial to the girl. Continuing to speak ill of her and referring to John's child as a bastard will not end well for you. Goodnight, Mrs. Hathaway."

She hung up the phone and looked toward the dining room. Laughter from within assured her the group continued to enjoy themselves, ignorant of Jeanette's latest ploy to stir up trouble in John's life.

~~~

Thursday, November 24, 1955

Sandra sat at the piano dredging up memories of her four years of taking lessons. Matt sat on a stool nearby with his guitar. The two had practiced together a few evenings over the last two months but had not become proficient playing together yet. However, the rest of the people gathered around singing along didn't notice. Hymns had been sung first. Now they were enjoying some rousing mountain tunes. Kathryn had produced a dulcimer for Earl to play, and he did his best to reproduce some of the music he created on one in his youth.

When the doorbell rang, followed by someone banging on the front door, it was Earl who set aside his instrument and hurried to answer it. "Well, hello, Jeanette. We weren't expecting you to drop in this afternoon."

Taken aback by the unexpected sight of Matt's father, she spit out, "What are you doing here?"

Earl's smile matched the one Jeanette hated seeing on his son. "Well, I was invited to spend the holiday here with my son and my late wife's family like I usually do. What's your reason for showing up?" He stepped back to allow her to enter. "Your husband isn't with you this evening?"

She stormed past without bothering to reply. Stomping down the stairs toward the great room, she followed the sounds until she stood staring at the heartwarming scene around the piano. "Was it necessary I find out from friends at the club that your wedding has been cancelled?"

John stepped forward before his grandmother could intercede. "The wedding has not been cancelled, Mother. We merely moved it to the church in Inverness as of last Friday. The date and time remain the same. I've been so busy with school and helping work out the logistical details of the change that I hadn't taken time to let you know yet. I apologize. However, I am confused about who told you it was cancelled and where they heard such a story."

Jeanette stared blankly from John to Sandra to Millie to Kathryn. "We dined today with the Daltons and Michaelsons. Paula Dalton said it was taken off the church calendar. If Winston and I hadn't spent the weekend elsewhere, I could have been humiliated at church last Sunday for knowing nothing about the cancellation." Anger overtook her as she finally understood why. "As it was, I looked stupid today because I knew nothing of it. Now I'll look stupid for not knowing it had simply been moved!"

Matt cleared his throat but remained quiet when his father scowled at him. Sandra rose and walked over to stand next to John. Greg stood, prepared to defend his sister from another attack if necessary. Kathryn remained seated but raised a hand to silence the others.

"Perhaps if you made some effort to join in the planning instead of defaming Sandra and your own son, you would not require special notification of details surrounding the wedding. Besides, you and I spoke only yesterday evening at which time I specifically referred to Sandra as John's fiancée and future bride. That does not indicate a cancelled wedding. Also, let me make something clear now, Mrs. Hathaway. If you cause a disturbance at the wedding or reception, I will make it my life's goal to repay you in kind. If you interfere in the wedding plans or with any other aspect of John and Sandra's life or that of their child, you will regret it for years to come. Do we understand one another?"

Jeanette's labored breathing made the only sound in the room as the two women glared at one another. "Yes, Mrs. Stuart. Fortunately, your time to belittle me, accuse me, torment me will end one day." She spun and stomped out of the room. Earl and Matt followed and stood together on the front steps as she sped away.

When they returned to the great room, Sandra held John's arm while she whispered to him. The rest of the family and friends tried to regain some of the lighthearted enjoyment from earlier. Kathryn stood and walked to John and Sandra. "I'm sorry, but I felt the time had come to ensure she understood her abuse and fits of pique would not be tolerated. You shall have the wedding you wish free of any drama from her, and you shall not be forced to worry that she might appear at any moment to harangue you either in public or in private. I do not expect her to remember my warning indefinitely, but she shall heed it for the foreseeable future. She slipped her arms around the couple and whispered a few more words before turning to the room. "Matt, would you provide some further entertainment for our family and guests? I need to retire to the study to see to some work."

Matt walked over and leaned down to kiss her cheek. "Yes, Aunt Kate, I'll be happy to do so." He took the opportunity to pat John on the shoulder before walking back to his guitar. "Any requests?" he asked as he slipped the strap over his head.

~~~

Friday, November 25, 1955

Sandra rushed through the front door, leaving John in her wake. "We got them! They're perfect!" She grabbed the railing and hurried down the steps as fast as she dared. At five months, she had begun to feel her center of gravity shifting forward. As much as she wanted to show off the wedding invitations, she wouldn't risk taking a tumble.

When she reached the bottom, she sped into the great room where Matt, Earl, and Kathryn chatted. She skidded to a halt in front of John's grandmother and slid a box from the pale green Greene's Stationery bag. Opening the box, she held it out for Kathryn to see the invitation on top. "It's just as pretty as I knew it would be, and they were so great to rush the new ones through so we could have them this weekend."

Kathryn picked up the ivory card and read it. "Very nice, dear. Why don't you catch your breath before we adjourn to the dining room to begin addressing them? Did you and John eat while you were in Elkford or would you need to have a little lunch before we start our work? Lila can make you two a sandwich."

"Thank you, Grandmother Kathryn, but we saw some of our friends and ate with them at the five and dime. I'll take my coat up and change shoes and then I'll be ready to begin addressing. Oh, Mother isn't here yet, is she?"

"No, but she should be any minute. Colonel Waters offered to check the radio in her car this morning. It wasn't picking up anything but static, and he said it's probably just a loose antenna wire."

"Oh, that's nice of him. I'll be right back." She breezed out of the room, passing John who had stopped to shed his own coat before trailing her into the great room.

In minutes, Sandra returned, invitation list in hand. "I have the names and addresses. Each of us addressing envelopes can have a page from it." She grabbed up the package of invitations from the coffee table and charged toward the dining room. When she reached the door, she turned back to face the others who had only begun to stand. Matt and Earl stopped to stretch and chat, and Sandra began tapping her foot. "I know you're trying to aggravate me, Matt. Get in here. You and Uncle Earl can stuff the envelopes."

Matt and Earl laughed and picked up their pace toward the dining room. Sandra began passing out pens and lists as the group assembled at last. Millie arrived minutes later, Vance with her, and she took a page before settling at the far end of the table.

Slowly, the pile of addressed envelopes grew. Matt was dispatched to the study to retrieve stamps, and he and Earl began the meticulous job of licking and placing the postage exactly one-sixteenth inch from the top and right edges.

Sandra picked up her notepad and flipped to another short list. This time, she began to write names on a handful of envelopes which would require no address. When she completed the first two, she stood and walked around the table behind Matt and Earl. She held out the two envelopes, each bearing only their respective names, planting a kiss on each one's cheek. "Thank you for all you've done for us. I appreciate your support more than I'll ever be able to tell you." She prepared another and took it to Vance. "Thank you, too, Colonel Waters. Without you, I wouldn't be able to finish high school. You've been so great to help us in other ways, too, and I can't thank you enough. We would love for you to spend our wedding day with us if you plan to be in Elkford at the time."

Vance took the offered envelope, stealing a look at Millie. "I would be pleased to attend your wedding. You have been one of the best students I've taught, and it has been a pleasure getting to know you and your family, Sandra."

"Thank you, Colonel. I hope I can maintain my focus on my schoolwork over the next few weeks. I'm afraid the wedding will make it harder and harder, but I'll try." She returned to her seat and wrote names on two more envelopes before disappearing into the kitchen to search for Lila and Mary. When she returned, she said, "John, would you get the other package?"

He rose and walked out to the hall to retrieve a bag from the table. Returning, he took out two small, double, silver frames. "When we tried to determine how best to handle my mother with regard to whether she would expect or want an invitation as mother of the groom, we came up with what we hope will be a good middle ground. We liked the idea so much we decided to get two more."

Sandra passed John an invitation and took one of the frames. Each put an invitation into a frame. John held one out to his grandmother, and Sandra walked around to give the other to her mother. "We'll put a photograph from our wedding in the other side when we get them," Sandra said. She hugged Millie, both allowing a few tears to trickle down their cheeks. "Thank you for everything you've done for me. I know it's been a difficult time, but your support has meant everything to us and made things so much easier than they would have been otherwise."

John and Kathryn shared a silent moment together before he moved around to hug Millie also, and Sandra hurried around to his grandmother. "Thank you, Grandmother Kathryn. None of this would be possible without your help," Sandra whispered as she hugged the elderly woman.

"It has been my pleasure, dear. As good a match as I thought you would make for John a few months ago, I have become even more convinced as you have dealt with the obstacles presented to you in coping with your pregnancy, planning the wedding, and facing opposition from numerous quarters. I am thrilled that John will spend his life with you and that you will be the mother of his children."

Sandra wiped at her eyes before hugging the matriarch again. "Thank you. You cannot imagine how much I appreciate knowing you feel that way."

Chapter 17

Saturday, November 26, 1955

Several horses waited on the driveway, snorting and pawing the ground in impatience. Bells hung from their saddles. Jonah's truck idled nearby, a collection of ropes, saws, and tarps in the bed and an empty trailer hooked behind. A host of other vehicles belonging to various residents of Chestnut Cove crowded the looping driveway. Each sported red and green ribbons flying from antennas, door handles, and anywhere else someone could find to attach them.

When Kathryn emerged from the house decked out in a red wool coat, she waved to the assembled crowd. "Is everyone here, John?"

"Yes, ma'am, at least one person from each family," he replied.

"All right, let's go then." She crossed to Jonah's truck and climbed into the passenger seat. Mary already sat in the middle. Jonah closed Kathryn's door and hurried around to the driver's side.

Matt grabbed the reins of his horse and bounded into the saddle. Earl, John, and Greg followed suit. Sandra and Millie got into Vance's waiting car. A quick check assured John everyone was set, and he waved Matt forward. The horses took off at a brisk trot, bells jingling. Jonah pulled into line behind them with the other vehicles trailing. They wound their way along the driveway from the promontory where the house perched to the main road along the east side of the cove. While much of the center of the cove had been cleared for pasture and farming, vast swaths of trees encompassed most of the Stuart properties. Cut only as needed for the furniture manufacturing facility the Stuarts owned in Elkford, fence posts, firewood, and so forth, they maintained the majority of the old-growth forests on the estate.

Today would mark the only other reason trees were harvested each year: Christmas tree cutting day. Each family on the estate, all employed by or related to the Stuarts, would select a tree, and the men would cut and load them. For those deep in the woods in areas inaccessible by vehicle and too far to be carried out, Earl and the boys would truss them up with rope and canvas and drag them to the road with the horses.

The parade wound its way around until it crossed the bridge and exited the gates of the cove and moved onward to the main road. They followed the state road through the mountains for half a mile until they forked off onto another Stuart road which led to an area filled with fir and spruce trees. The horses came to a halt, and Jonah eased to a stop behind them. The other vehicles pulled to the side of the road, and families piled out and scrambled into the woods. There, interspersed among the towering, old-growth firs, smaller trees had been carefully cultivated over the years for this annual event.

Matt and Earl pushed forward on their horses, keeping an eye on the groups and remaining close to assist when necessary. Greg hopped down from his mount and tied it to Jonah's trailer where it could reach one of the buckets of water. John did likewise before assisting his grandmother from the truck.

"Do you want to walk out there to look for a tree this year, Gramma, or do you want the rest of us to pick one for the house?"

"I'll walk a short distance, but only to visit with some of the tenants. You and the others know how to select a tree for us. Don't forget you and Sandra need one for the carriage house, also, though you might not want to cut it yet."

"We talked about that. We only want a very small one, so I think we'll choose it today but come back to cut it closer to Christmas." He rubbed his temple when he remembered another task. "I need to cut one for Mother and Winston, too. I plan to take it to them this afternoon along with the framed wedding invitation."

"I assumed you would select their tree since they didn't attend today." She slipped her hand through his arm. "Let us join the others. You should speak to a few of the staff and then join Sandra."

"Yes, ma'am." They walked into the woods and visited with a couple of families who already located suitable trees near the road. John helped cut one before leading his grandmother deeper into the forest. A jingling alerted them to the return of one of the horses.

Matt appeared, trailing a canvas-encased spruce. "This one's for Lila and Mary. Jonah's cutting one for his folks now. How are we doing up here?"

"Two cut and loaded that we know of. Have you seen Sandra and Millie?"

"No, but we've been busy cutting. We spotted one we think would be good for us. It's about four-hundred feet northeast of here if you want to see it, Aunt Kate. I can bring John's mount if you want to ride back in there. I need to water mine before I go back for another tree."

"No, dear, I believe I'll turn back now if you'll escort me as you take Lila's tree." She reached out and took hold of the bridle.

Matt slid off and waved for John to go ahead to search for Sandra. "I'll boost you up if you want to ride, Aunt Kate."

"No, dear, I'm fine walking. The ground isn't too difficult." She shifted her hold from the horse's tack to Matt's arm.

Assured his cousin would see Kathryn back to the truck, John continued forward, stopping to assist and visit as he passed Gus and his family. When he located Sandra, Greg had ax in hand chopping at the base of the Duncan's tree while Vance held it steady.

John stopped beside Sandra, placing an arm around her shoulders. "Do you need me to go get one of the horses to haul it out of here?"

"I think we can carry it, don't you, Greg?" Vance said.

Greg took one last whack, and the tree teetered over in Vance's grasp. "We can manage between us. It isn't that big."

"All right," John said. "I think everyone else has a tree picked out, and some already have them cut. May I steal Sandra and start scouting for Gramma Kate's tree? Matt said he and Uncle Earl spotted a good candidate."

"Of course, John," Millie replied. "Where is she? Back in the truck?"

"Should be by now. Matt was escorting her back with Lila and Mary's tree." He took Sandra's hand, and they set off on their search. "Are you warm enough?"

"I'm fine," Sandra replied. "It isn't very cold today. Come on. We need to check on the one for your grandmother and find one for your mother and maybe for us."

When they reached the area to which Matt directed John, they found the tree with red ribbon tied around it. John held up his pocket tape to measure the height. "Just under ten feet, and it's a good diameter and full. What do you think?"

"I think it's perfect," Sandra said. "Should we go ahead and start cutting it or do you need someone to hold it? I'm afraid I'm not tall enough to help much on one so tall."

"Let's get Matt or Uncle Earl to help. I don't want to damage it. Besides, I'll need help getting it out of here. I need to trim the lowest branches first anyway."

"I'll walk back to find one of them while you do that."

By the time she returned with Matt astride John's horse, the tree was ready to cut. John and Matt felled and wrapped it, allowing Matt to begin the trek back to Jonah's trailer.

"All right, now we need to get one for your mother. I saw a small one which might work for our little apartment while I was walking. It's just off the path. I tied a ribbon on it so I can find it again and let you see what you think about it." Sandra slipped her hand in John's, and they started back through the woods.

~~~

Later that afternoon, John and Sandra drove to his mother's cottage. The top of the tree he cut for them protruded from the trunk of his Ford. Sandra fidgeted with the ribbon she had put around the framed invitation. She hadn't been to the Hathaway cottage often and not once since the revelation of her pregnancy. She had rarely even been in company with Jeanette since that time, and never without several people close to intervene should the woman become enraged. This time, she would only have John.

They pulled into the driveway, and John squeezed her hand. "Don't worry. Gramma just warned her to behave a couple of days ago. She'll be fine. Besides, we'll only be here long enough to bring in the tree and put it in the stand and give her the framed invitation."

Sandra forced a smile. "It will be fine. I'm just a little nervous. Come on." She opened her door and stepped out.

John retrieved the tree and followed her to the kitchen door. Sandra tapped on it and stepped back. Jeanette knew they were to deliver the tree about two o'clock, and John had reminded her to get the stand from the closet where the decorations were stored so it would be ready for him.

When Winston opened the door, Sandra relaxed slightly. "Good afternoon, Mr. Hathaway. We've brought your Christmas tree."

Winston pushed open the screen door and stepped back for Sandra to enter. John followed with the tree and led the group into the living room.

Jeanette sat on the sofa, hands in her lap. "Hello, John. It's kind of you to cut and bring us a tree. Winston, would you help him set it up? Do be careful of the knickknacks on the table."

Sandra stood to the side and watched John struggle to fit the tree into its stand while Winston fumbled uselessly to help. At last, the trunk slipped into place, and Winston managed to turn the screws the correct direction to tighten them. Steeling herself, Sandra walked forward and stopped in front of her future mother-in-law.

"Mrs. Hathaway?" Jeanette finally looked at Sandra. "Mrs. Hathaway, we brought you a small gift." She held out the picture frame. "It has one of our wedding invitations in one side. We'll give you a photograph of us from our wedding to put in the other side." She stopped and nibbled on her lip, waiting for Jeanette to take the offered item. "I know you aren't happy about any of this, but I hope one day you'll decide I'm a good wife to John and mother to his children."

The tree finally secure and straight in its stand, John moved to Sandra's side and put his arm around her waist. Jeanette pressed her lips together, her face showing her displeasure, but she held out her hand and took the offering. "Thank you."

"We need to get back to Gramma's to decorate the tree. I'll stop back here sometime next week," John said. Jeanette merely nodded.

Sandra turned away and pulled a handkerchief from her coat pocket. John put a hand on her back, and they retreated through the kitchen. As soon as John pulled the door closed behind them, Sandra choked out, "She's never going to accept me. I hate this part, John. I don't want to be responsible for coming between you and your mother."

He opened the car door and helped her inside before bending down to kiss her. "She's the one causing the problem, Sandra. I think she'll come around, but it will take time. At least she didn't say anything mean today."

"No, she didn't say a thing. She ignored me until you came over. At least she took the framed invitation. Maybe one day she'll appreciate it. I hope so."

Chapter 18

Saturday, December 10, 1955

A sliver of the Moon shone through the trees to the east. Otherwise, chilly darkness enveloped the house. The sun would not rise for more than an hour. A careful hand touched the doorknob, twisting it ever so slowly to withdraw the bolt. A soft giggle was cut short. A faint clink sounded far below. Soft slippers shuffled on the oak floor.

The door burst open. "Happy birthday!" shouted Matt, Sandra, and Mary. They piled into John's bedroom, tossing bits of paper confetti as they crossed the room and sprawled across the bed.

John, already sitting up, laughed. "You three would make terrible spies. I heard you coming for a mile."

Matt held up his hand with the last of the confetti and sprinkled it over John's head. "It's the girls, not me. They can't help giggling."

On cue, Sandra giggled. "You got in your share, too, Matt." She stole a look at the bedroom door before leaning over to kiss John. "Happy eighteenth birthday. I love you."

He slid his arms around her to more thoroughly claim his first present of the day.

"Hey, you two, time for that later." Matt tugged a pillow free and bashed John's arm with it. "Lila will have the biscuits in the oven. We need to get downstairs soon. First we need to help John clean up his mess."

The lovebirds broke apart, and Sandra began brushing the paper from John's hair. He picked up a few pieces and tossed them back toward Matt. "I didn't have a mess until you made one."

"And your point is?"

John snatched a pillow and swatted Matt with it. Mary and Sandra jumped clear and stood back watching the boys whack one another with their weapons of choice until the combatants collapsed on the bed laughing.

"I need to get back downstairs to help Mother," Mary said. "I'll see you down there." She slipped away, and Sandra followed her out, leaving the boys gasping for breath.

At just after seven o'clock, Matt paraded into the dining room doing his best impression of a bugle. His fanfare complete, he announced, "All rise to welcome the newest adult at Chestnut Cove." Dutifully, Sandra and Mary stood. To the astonishment of none, Kathryn rose from her seat at the head of the table, smiling at the antics of the youngsters. Even Lila, though already standing, stopped in the doorway to the kitchen in recognition of the solemn event.

Kathryn pointed to the far end of the table. "As the official man of the house now, why don't you take the place at the foot of the table. You'll need to wait until I'm gone to move to the head, of course." She chuckled at John's expression.

He bypassed the indicated seat to take his normal spot to her right, kissing her cheek before he sat. "Thank you, Gramma, but I prefer to stay at this end with you." A shadow passed over his face, though he kept a smile in place. He had seen his grandfather and father sit at one end of that table and lost both. He had suffered through countless tense meals in the presence of his mother and grandmother watching them volley veiled insults back and forth. While he appreciated the gesture and understood the love behind it, he had no interest in taking a lead position at that table. He doubted he ever would.

Once everyone had filled their plate, Kathryn said, "It is rather cold out today. What plans do you have, John, other than dinner tonight?"

"We want to finish arranging the furniture in the carriage house and maybe move a few personal things over there like our books. Sandra and I both have a collection of those. We'd like to have it ready to move in before the last week of wedding preparations. Maybe even move our summer clothes over there since there's no chance we'll need those in the next two weeks." A gust of wind sailing down the length of the cove wailed as it whipped past the house, emphasizing his point.

"Just remember to save space for the wedding gifts you are likely to receive. You can always add things like lamps and knickknacks such as candleholders later. Have you and Sandra discussed my offered gift to you?"

He turned to smile at Sandra as he answered. "Yes, ma'am, it's very generous of you, but it's too much with what you've already done for us."

"Nonsense," Kathryn responded. She set her fork down and picked up her coffee. "You will soon have a new baby, and you will be off to college some distance from here. You require more reliable transportation. I insist you select something suitable. You should keep your current car since you and Sandra will each require a vehicle at times, and it is still serviceable. However, I insist you two have something newer at your disposal. Since it will serve as a combination gift for both of you for your birthdays and graduation, it is hardly excessive. Perhaps if the temperature rises and the wind decreases later in the morning, you and Sandra could go into Elkford and look at what the dealers have available. I admit today is not the most pleasant for browsing their lots."

"All right, Gramma, we'll go look at them, though maybe not today unless the weather improves. Since we're not going away on a honeymoon, we can spend time the week after Christmas looking at cars if we don't get an opportunity to do so before then."

The phone rang, ending the discussion for the moment. Lila went to answer it and returned frowning. "Mrs. Hathaway says they are without water."

John groaned. "I bet neither of them remembered to check the wellhouse the last few days. Last night was the coldest of the season. The pipes probably froze. I'll go check it."

He slid his chair back, but Kathryn put a hand on his to stop him. "No, John, you will not. It is my tenants' responsibility to properly maintain their wellhouses in the winter once I've had someone check them before the first freeze. You shall not go out in this cold and wind to try to make repairs, and neither shall any member of my staff. The weather is much too severe to deal with water pipes."

"But Gramma..."

"No, John. They must learn to manage for themselves at some point. Next winter, you will be in Coughton except during breaks from school. Should you leave your wife and child and skip examinations to hurry to your mother's cottage because she and her husband cannot remember to do a simple task such as checking the wellhouse blanket and light? They will not perish. We will send water if they lack any to drink. The roads are quite dry and passable, so they may drive into Elkford easily for anything they need, including a motel room until the weather improves enough for someone to effect repairs in decent weather."

John glanced across the table at Matt. His cousin sat back with arms crossed. No support would be forthcoming from him. "All right, Gramma. Why don't I take them water and spend a few minutes there since it's my birthday? I promise I won't do any work on their well pipes. As cold as it is, they're probably frozen solid anyway and nothing can be done right now."

Matt pushed back his chair. "I'll ride with you to help carry the water." His unspoken second task would be to ensure John didn't attempt any repairs.

~~~

Jeanette's glowing smile faded into a deep scowl as soon as she saw Matt standing behind John.

John held up one of the steel cans he carried. "We brought four five-gallon containers of water, Mother. Did anyone remember to check the wellhouse in the last few days? I'm afraid the pipes probably froze solid in this cold weather. It was nineteen this morning when I checked the thermometer. If they froze, there's nothing anyone can do until it warms up. At least you'll have plenty of water to drink and to wash with in the meantime."

Matt trailed him into the kitchen and set his burden in a corner. "Aunt Kate said the Mountain View Motel should have plenty of rooms available if you and Winston would rather stay there with running water for the next week until it warms up some. You won't be able to get a plumber to come up and work on well piping until it's warmer."

Jeanette understood the message. Kathryn would not issue an invitation to stay at the main house until their water issue was resolved, and the responsibility for repairs due to their negligence rested solely with the tenants. She seethed in silence and stomped into the living room where a package wrapped in blue paper waited on the coffee table. She snatched it up and shoved it into John's hands. "Happy birthday, John. I'm sorry I won't be afforded an opportunity to spend more than a few minutes with my only child on such an auspicious day."

He took the gift and kissed her cheek. "We'll make up for it next year, Mother. It's been a very hectic last few weeks. Shall I open this now?"

"As you please." She sat on the sofa, and John took a place next to her. Matt didn't wait for the invitation he knew would never come to sit on a chair across from them.

John peeled off the paper and opened the box beneath. He held up a navy wool sweater with the Coughton Tech logo. "Thank you, Mother. I'll enjoy wearing it at school this year as well as at Coughton next winter."

"Then you still plan to attend Coughton next fall? Since I rarely hear firsthand information about you anymore, I could only assume that had not changed."

"Yes, Mother, those plans remain unchanged other than now Sandra and the baby will go with me." As if searching for a safe topic, he looked around the living room. "Mother, there's little coal on the hearth. Is there more inside or should we bring some in for you? I know you don't like using the fireplace, but if the electricity goes out in this wind and cold, you'll need to rely on the coal to keep the house warm until they can restore power."

Matt stood and waved for John to remain seated. Certain his cousin would not offer to go out in the freezing weather to try to solve the water issue today, the least Matt could do was bring in a couple of buckets of coal while John spent a few moments alone with his mother.

When he completed his task, Matt resumed his seat. After a few more minutes of awkward small talk, John rose and ended the visit none of the three enjoyed.

~~~

Monday, December 12, 1955

John had ridden to school with Matt that morning. When he walked out to the parking lot at the end of the day, a short search found his grandmother's car waiting. He gave Matt a quick wave and hurried to the black Cosmopolitan, Millie behind the wheel. He slid into the back and planted a big kiss on Sandra's lips. "I haven't been able to concentrate all day." Belatedly, he leaned forward. "Hello, Gramma Kate, Mrs. Duncan. How are you this afternoon?"

"We're all well, dear, but I am concerned by your comment. Did you do poorly on your math test?"

Shaking his head, John said, "No, I think I did all right, but I couldn't begin to tell you what we talked about in history or English. I took notes, but I wasn't concentrating. I'll check Matt's to see if I missed anything important. I was just too excited about this afternoon." He sat back and returned his attention to Sandra. "Did you do any better with Colonel Waters today? He gave you a history test, right?"

She slid her hand through his arm and scooted closer. "I got a ninety-six. I also did well on the book report I finished last week. I only have one more to complete to have all those out of the way, and I'm halfway done reading the book already."

"How can you concentrate today? All I could think about was going to the courthouse to start the paperwork for our marriage license." He leaned forward again. "Gramma, are you sure the doctor's office will stay open in case we get held up at the courthouse?"

Kathryn chuckled. "Yes, dear, they know we might not get there until just after five o'clock and will wait for us. I believe you will be the most eager patient they've ever had to get a blood test."

Millie started the car and fell into line with the students trying to escape the school. They had progressed almost to the exit when a jolt and the crunch of metal shocked them. John grabbed Sandra and held her until he was sure nothing further would happen.

"Is anyone hurt?" Kathryn asked.

"We're fine, Gramma," John replied. "Are you two OK?"

Millie nodded and opened her door. The others followed suit. A young man climbed from his car just behind them, apologizing profusely. Rachel Pullen exited the passenger side of his car.

"Oh, what a shame you might not get to the courthouse in time," she gushed to John. "Oh, hi, Sandra. It's so nice to see you. You've put on some weight since I saw you last."

John started toward Rachel's boyfriend. Despite his apologies, he couldn't hide a smirk at her greeting to Sandra. John knew the hit had been deliberate. Before he could reach the boy, Matt rushed up to them to prevent any fisticuffs. Greg followed, as did Perry and several other friends. Within seconds, they attracted a sizable crowd of onlookers, further clogging the route for exiting vehicles.

Matt pressed his keys into John's hand. "Here, take my car. It's near the back of the line. Take Sandra and Millie and go out the other way. Let Aunt Kate and me handle this. Don't let them cause you and Sandra to not get your license today. That's what they're trying to do. They've stepped over a line deliberately hitting Aunt Kate's car. The principal and the sheriff can punish them, John."

Kathryn appeared from around the other side of the cars. "He's right, John. There's a proper way to deal with this. Don't get into a fight. Go ahead and take Sandra and Millie. They're the ones who need to be with you at the courthouse. Do you have the money for the license and doctor with you?"

John tore his attention from the boy, forcing his hands to relax their clinch. "Yes, Gramma, I know you're right." He took one last look back at Rachel and her stooge. "You'll be sorry."

Rachel laughed, and the boy took a step toward John, but the voice of the principal stopped him in his tracks. He pointed at Rachel and the boy. "Go to my office and wait. Both of you." When the teens finally moved away, he took a quick look at the cars, still bumper to bumper. "I'm so sorry, Mrs. Stuart. I'll see to it his parents learn of his carelessness."

"I believe you will find that it was anything but careless," Kathryn said. "But first, John and Sandra are due at the courthouse now. Do you have any issue with them and Mrs. Duncan, who was driving my car, leaving in Matt's to attend their business while we await the sheriff?"

The man blinked. "Uh, sheriff? Um, no, they may go ahead since clearly Mrs. Duncan was not at fault."

Kathryn waved the others on. "Go ahead, John. Matt and Greg and I will be along in my car once this is dealt with. I believe my car is drivable, do you not agree, Matt?"

Matt straightened from an examination of the underside of her Cosmopolitan. "Yes, Aunt Kate. It's just a bent bumper and brackets. Nothing else looks damaged. The dealer should be able to get new parts shipped to Elkford in a few days to repair it."

"Very well. John, take Millie and Sandra and get your license."

At last, John took Sandra's hand and hurried toward Matt's car, Millie following them.

Chapter 19

Tuesday, December 20, 1955

The last week had been calm. The license was procured, the car repaired, and two students severely disciplined, though the last had no direct impact on the Stuart and Duncan families other than the satisfaction it brought them.

More important to the residents of Chestnut Cove, today began the final push toward the wedding. Cindy and Calvin had arrived late in the afternoon. As soon as they unloaded their luggage at Millie's, the Duncans and Cal hurried to the main house for dinner.

When the doorbell rang, Sandra did her best to rush up the stairs to open the front door. The sisters squealed and cried as they babbled, catching up with every step back to the great room. Matt stood in the background enjoying the spectacle while John moved forward to greet his future in-laws. At Kathryn's nod, Matt went into the kitchen to tell Lila she could begin the last of her dinner preparations. Fifteen minutes later, Kathryn had John and Sandra lead the group into the dining room.

They had nearly finished their meal when the telephone rang. Mary slipped away to answer it. Within seconds, she raced back into the room. "Excuse me, Mrs. Stuart, but it's an emergency. There's a fire at your canvas company. Mr. Bertram is on the telephone."

Kathryn rose and hurried to speak to the man. "Mr. Bertram, how severe is it? Is everyone out of the building? Has the fire department begun to contain it?"

"Everyone is out. Thankfully we only have a skeleton crew this week. The fire brigade has deployed their equipment and put water on it, but it isn't under control yet," he replied. "It's the warehouse in the center of the complex. I'm concerned it could spread to both the mill and the manufacturing building."

"I understand, Mr. Bertram. I shall be there shortly. Where are you located?"

"In the sales office across the street, but I may need to move should the fire chief decide this area is in danger."

"Do as you must to remain safe. If you aren't there when I arrive, I shall find you." When she hung up, Matt, John, and Millie surrounded her, waiting for further details. "John, you shall take over as host. Matt, I am afraid I shall require you to drive me into Elkford. The finished canvas goods warehouse is afire, and thus far the firemen have not brought it under control."

"Of course, Aunt Kate. I'll get our coats." Matt rushed upstairs, leaving John and Millie with Kathryn.

"Gramma, I need to go with you," John said.

"Under other circumstances, I would agree. However, tonight you must remain here with Sandra's family. Matt and I will be fine. One of us will call with an update when we know something more." She hugged him and gave him a gentle nudge toward the dining room where Sandra and the rest waited for more information. "Millie, you and Lila continue with the dress fittings after dinner as planned. I may require a little of your assistance tomorrow, though I will not allow anything to interfere appreciably with the wedding preparations."

"Of course, Mrs. Stuart. Please take care tonight."

"We will, my dear." Matt had returned, and he held out Kathryn's warmest coat while she slipped her arms into it. He took her hand, and they hurried up the steps to the foyer as quickly as the seventy-nine-year-old woman could.

As soon as Matt wheeled the car away from the house, he asked the inevitable question. "Do you think this could be arson?"

"I hope to know that answer in the future, but for now I can only speculate. We have tried to minimize fire hazards in the warehouse and the other buildings in the complex, and only a few people were present today. There should be little to cause a fire other than carelessness or a deliberate act."

"That's what I thought, Aunt Kate."

~~~

When Matt placed a call to the house from the suite above the sales office two hours later, John answered on the first ring.

"They've gotten it under control," Matt said, "but the warehouse will be a total loss. The other buildings appear to be safe."

"Good. How's Gramma?"

"She's fine. She's downstairs in the sales office talking to Mr. Bertram and the fire chief, but she wanted me to come upstairs to Uncle Alistair's old office to call you with an update. I'll make sure she sits and rests while she waits for more information. I don't think she'll leave until the fire is out."

"No, I wouldn't think so. At least she has somewhere inside to sit out of the cold and the smoke."

"Well, it's warm for now, but they cut off the gas in this area because of the fire. It will get chilly inside, but we're out of the wind and the fire's heat has limited the cold around here so far. I might try to talk her into going home later and letting me stay here with Mr. Bertram. I'll let you know if I talk her into that so you can come get her."

"I hope she'll agree. I can bring blankets and pillows so you and Mr. Bertram can stay warm while you wait."

"Did the ladies finish their dress fittings? Aunt Kate wanted me to ask."

"Yes, Sandra said everything is fine. The Duncans are still here waiting for an update on the fire. I think they'll go home once I tell them what you've passed on so they can get some rest. Millie went into the study and pulled the insurance papers for the canvas business. They're waiting on the desk."

"I'll let her know. I hear someone coming up the stairs. I'll call later with an update."

Matt hung up and met Kathryn at the top of the steps. "Anything new?"

"Only that they expect to have the fire out soon." She eased down into a chair and stretched out her legs. "Did you reach John?"

"Yes, ma'am, I updated him on the fire. He said the dress fitting went well, and Millie located the insurance paperwork you'll need tomorrow." He sat on the edge of the desk. "Aunt Kate, John will come get you later if you'll let me stay here tonight with Mr. Bertram to keep an eye on things for you. I know you won't go yet, but I hope you won't stay all night."

She reached out and took his hand. "I am aware I'm not young, Matt. I may take you and John up on your offer once the fire is completely out."

Matt stood and walked across to the window. The warehouse remnants still glowed orange, but the night sky was no longer filled with bits of flaming canvas. The masonry walls and steel roofs on the mill and manufacturing facility served them well in preventing those structures from catching fire.

"Does the fire department have any more information about where it started or how?"

"They believe it began along the east wall, but they don't have anything further yet." She closed her eyes as she spoke. "There are windows along that wall. Someone could access the building from the river side without being seen."

"Yes, ma'am, they aren't too high to get in. Even easier to break a window and throw in a container of gasoline and a lit rag."

~~~

When the Stuart telephone rang again, John wondered who it could be. Matt had called less than fifteen minutes earlier. There's no way he could have convinced Kathryn Stuart to leave already. Millie's family had left only minutes before, not enough time to get to her cottage and call for some reason. "Hello?"

"Oh, John, I was afraid that woman had dragged you into Elkford tonight."

"Mother, what are you talking about?"

"The fire, John. Winston and I had dinner at the club and heard the whole mill had burned to the ground."

John took a seat in his grandmother's chair in the great room. "No, only the warehouse in the middle of the block. That's bad enough though. It's a total loss. The mill and its warehouse to the south and the manufacturing building to the north are both safe."

"I'm sure you're wrong, John. Vaughn knew all about it. He said the whole complex would burn. There would be no way the fire department could stop it spreading from that central building."

"Well, they did. Gramma and Matt are there, and I just heard from Matt a few minutes ago." As he processed her words, he continued, "How did Mr. Michaelson know so much about it?"

"I presume he saw it on the way from his office to the club. He's very intelligent. He probably could tell how terrible it would be. I'm sure he's right and your grandmother is wrong."

John had learned when not to argue with her. "We'll know one way or another tomorrow morning, Mother. Did you have a nice dinner?"

"Yes, we did. They served prime rib, which Winston loves. Paula and Hoyt joined us. We asked Vaughn and Lilly, his new wife, to join us when they arrived, but they already planned to meet another couple. Besides, we were nearly done by then. She looked very pale. I'm not at all sure she's a healthy young woman."

John had learned all he was likely to from her, so he decided to end the call before she rambled too far afield. "I need to keep the line open in case Matt or Gramma needs to call. I'll talk to you tomorrow, Mother."

As soon as he hung up, he went into the study and closed the door to call his grandfather's office. When Matt answered, John said, "Hey, I just got a call from Mother. She and Winston dined at the club tonight and heard about the fire." He stopped to gather his thoughts. "She said something I thought you and Gramma should know. It might not mean anything, but Mr. Michaelson is the one who told them about the fire. He and his wife got to the club late, and he told her the complex would be a complete loss. He insisted the fire spread from the warehouse to the other buildings."

When Matt didn't reply after several seconds, John said, "Are you still there? Matt?"

"I'm here. I was just thinking."

"Yeah, me, too. Any more information about the fire? How and where it started?" John picked up a pencil and began to doodle on a pad of paper.

"Not how, but they think it started on the rear wall by the river. They won't be sure until it's completely out and the inspector views it in daylight."

"But Vaughn Michaelson acted like he knew all about it shortly after it started. Does Gramma suspect arson?"

"We've talked about the possibility. We didn't mention names, but I'm sure we both had him in mind."

John tapped the pencil on the desk. "You know, I'm almost sorry we don't go to the club much. It might be useful to cross paths with that man at times."

"Yep, he bears watching."

~~~

Wednesday, December 21, 1955

When Matt, Mr. Bertram, and the fire inspector walked through the warehouse remnants just after sunrise, they had a full view of the sky. Some of the rafters had burned, allowing part the roof to collapse. The rear wall had mostly collapsed also. Firemen continued to spray water on a few spots where heavier timbers still gave off heat on the cold winter morning.

The inspector said, "Mr. Bertram, your employee who first saw the smoke informed us it came from around here. This is also the area with the most destruction. That leads me to suspect this is where it began. Can you tell me what was in this part of the warehouse?"

Bertram looked around to get his bearings. "Completed tarpaulins stacked in wood racks."

"Is that the place with the most densely packed material in here?" Matt asked.

"Yes, I would say so," Bertram replied. "The tents would be of similar density, and they were on the next row to the west."

Matt pointed to a spot along the remnants of the east wall. "There were windows all along here."

The inspector looked around to get a feel for the warehouse layout prior to the fire, trying to compare it to his fire map of downtown Elkford. "A good entry point should someone intentionally start a fire. No one was working in this building yesterday?"

"No," Mr. Bertram said. "Only the maintenance crew is working this week, and they were only in the mill. No one had cause to enter this building. Our people are also well-trained not to smoke in the warehouses or the plants. They understand the danger."

While the men stood discussing possible causes of the fire, a shout and sudden flurry of activity along the riverbank south of the mill attracted their attention. A deputy hurried up moments later. "We found an empty, five-gallon gas can hung in the bushes along the river. It's about three-hundred yards upstream. It was in the water, but the cap had been closed, so it floated and hung up in some brush along the bank."

"Show us," the inspector said. Matt and Mr. Bertram followed the officials across the level ground between the warehouse remnants and the Wolf River south until they had passed along the back of the canvas mill. Another deputy stood atop the edge of the bank with a dented, red gasoline can at his feet.

The inspector opened the cap and sniffed. "No doubt it held gasoline." He leaned over the edge to look down. "Hung right out there?"

"Yes, sir," the second deputy said. "I climbed down and fetched it. Somebody must have tossed it out there expecting it to sink or float away."

Matt mumbled, "Somebody who didn't realize the river flowed north–right back the way he had just come if he was fleeing the warehouse after setting the fire–or else he didn't realize he had the cap tight enough to keep it from filling with water and sinking."

The inspector smiled at the young man's perception. "Most people don't realize an empty steel gasoline can will float if the cap's tight."

"I don't suppose there's any chance of finding fingerprints after it's been in the water?"

"We'll try, but it's unlikely, and there's no guarantee this can is connected to the fire. It's a good chance though. Doesn't look like the can's been floating long." He looked back toward the remnants of the warehouse. "We'll be asking around for anyone who saw somebody in this area last night or anyone with a gas can nearby. It's doubtful since it's secluded back here and it happened well after dark, but we might get lucky. Meantime, I need to get back over there to look for more clues. Tell Mrs. Stuart I hope to have a best guess about what happened by the end of the day."

"Yes, sir. Thank you."

The inspector and Mr. Bertram returned to the warehouse. The deputies resumed their search of the riverbank behind the Stuart canvas complex. Matt remained in place, scanning the surrounding area. Satisfied he had learned all he could from that position, he circled around the south side of the canvas mill and crossed the street to the sales office. Stopping in front of it, he again took in everything within sight. Finally, he walked northward and crossed back to the burned-out warehouse.

Chapter 20

Greg tugged at the collar of his shirt, earning him a scowl from his eldest sister.

"Quit fussing with it, Greg," Cindy said. "Tomorrow will be worse, so you might as well get used to it now. It's no tighter than any Sunday at church."

"Yeah, but I don't have to walk down the aisle with everybody watching on Sundays."

Cindy reached out and loosened the offending noose enough to allow him to breathe easier. "I have news for you, Greg. Nobody will even notice you tomorrow. They'll only see the bride. Speaking of the bride, where's Sandra?"

"She and John are talking to Reverend McPherson in his office," Matt said. He had abandoned his post at the front of the church to wander back to the narthex where the rest of the wedding party waited. "They wanted to go over a few details of the ceremony with him first before the rest of us are standing up there doing nothing."

"Well, it isn't like we can do the full rehearsal yet. Mother and Mrs. Stuart and your father still aren't here. I hope they're done speaking to the fire marshal and sheriff and are on the way here." She tugged Greg's tie straighter, then snuck a look outside. "Do you think Mrs. Hathaway will come today?"

With a shrug, Matt said, "I don't have any idea, but I hope not. The only thing she has to do is walk down the aisle to be seated." He patted his coat pocket. "That reminds me, Dad and I need somebody to hold these when the coast is clear." He produced two pieces of hay, one about an inch shorter than the other. "Someone has to escort her to her seat, either Dad or me. The other gets Aunt Kate." He gave Greg a friendly punch in the shoulder. "You get lucky. You get your mother and your sister."

"I have to escort them both?" the youth choked out. "Why me?"

"Silly boy," Cindy said. Suddenly unhappy with his tie again, she tugged it tighter. "That's what you did when Cal and I married. If you don't want to escort Mother, Cal can do that part. He's helping seat guests like Matt's father. Just remember, nobody pays attention to anyone but the bride. Besides, at the ripe old age of fifteen, you'll be done escorting ladies down the church aisle."

Matt flashed a grin. "Well, unless he has a passel of daughters one day. Then he can start all over when they get married."

"I'm never getting married or having kids," Greg grumbled.

Further harassment of the boy ended when Gwen flew in. "All right, the bride and groom are ready. Still no sign of Kathryn and Millie and Earl?"

"No, not yet," Matt replied. "Can we practice the part at the front with just us?"

"Yes, that's the main thing to work out. We'll begin with the bridesmaid's entry and continue from there. The seating of the mothers and grandmother shouldn't be a problem to work out. Come along, let's talk at the altar a moment and then we'll begin."

The group met John, Sandra, and the minister at the front of the sanctuary and began working through the details of the ceremony. They had run through it twice when the door opened, and Jeanette stepped inside.

John broke off to greet her before introducing her to the minister. "Mother, this is Reverend McPherson and his wife, Gwen."

"I believe we've met, though it's been some years, Mrs. Hathaway. It's nice to see you." Gwen extended her hand, and Jeanette shook it. "We've just finished rehearsing the actual ceremony. We're ready to walk through the entry of the bride and the rest of the wedding party, though Mrs. Stuart and Mrs. Duncan aren't here yet." She took Jeanette's elbow and guided her back down the aisle. "What color dress have you chosen to wear to your son's wedding, Mrs. Hathaway? I'm sure you've selected something fashionable."

While Gwen was doing her best to soothe Jeanette and prevent an outburst of some kind without Kathryn on hand to manage the situation, the black Cosmopolitan pulled into the church parking lot. Earl hopped out of the driver's seat and went around to escort Kathryn. Millie climbed from the back and followed them into the church.

"Oh, Kathryn, there you are," Gwen gushed. "We finished practicing the ceremony and were about to walk everyone through the seating. Come along and we'll do that quickly so you can get to the other things you need to do today. I know everyone is busy with last-minute preparations, plus you're dealing with that awful fire."

"Hello, Gwen. We're sorry to be late, but there was no alternative. They needed a few details about the business Mr. Bertram couldn't provide." Kathryn shifted her attention to Jeanette. "I'm pleased to see you here, Mrs. Hathaway. Will you and Mr. Hathaway join us for dinner tonight? I know how fond you are of dining at the country club, and I felt I needed to relieve Lila of preparing dinner for so many tonight when she needs to prepare the cake and some of the reception food for tomorrow. I was most thankful the club could accommodate us on short notice."

"We already planned to dine there tonight. We shall join your party for a short time at least." Jeanette's pinched face declared her lack of enthusiasm.

"Excellent. All right, Gwen, tell us what we need to know for tomorrow, and we shall walk through the seating, although if it is all the same to you, I believe I shall stand for today. I've had quite enough sitting already listening to the various authorities speak on the results of their investigation into the fire."

Gwen charged into the details of seating the bride and groom's families. When discussion came to the order, Kathryn made it clear she would be seated prior to Jeanette, per normal order, and not try to usurp the groom's mother as next to last to take her seat.

As soon as they finished the rehearsal, Jeanette hurried away, and Matt and John trailed Kathryn out of the church, eager for an update concerning the fire. "Did they decide it was arson? Do they have any suspects?" John asked.

"Yes, they are satisfied someone set the fire," Kathryn answered. She stopped at the front of her car and looked around to ensure no one outside immediate family could hear their conversation. "However, they have identified no suspects or found any evidence to point them in a direction likely to identify one. Though no one believes we had anything to do with it, the insurance company may balk at paying the claim because of the arson clause in the policy. My attorney will handle it, but I fear we may not recoup the cost of the building. However, that is an issue to worry over later. For now, it is out of our hands."

Matt shook his head in frustration. "Do we need to post extra guards in case someone comes back to try to burn the rest of the canvas complex or the furniture company or any of the other Stuart interests? I don't suppose you mentioned anything about Mr. Michaelson pushing you to sell property you don't want to sell or someone blackmailing the minister. It sure sounded like Michaelson knew a lot about the fire in a hurry Tuesday night. I walked all around the surrounding area trying to see what could have misled him to think the whole complex would burn. I believe he just expected it to because he knew something."

"Perhaps, but that is speculation. You know that, Matt. He's never made an overt threat to me I could report to the sheriff, and it is not for me to sully the Reverend's name regardless of how farfetched the accusation against him. The sheriff will have his men keep a close eye on things for now as a precaution, and Mr. Bertram is calling a few of our longtime workers to ask if each will take a shift keeping watch over the holidays. However, I doubt anything further will be attempted in the next few days. To do so would convince the District Attorney that someone deliberately targeted our holdings and bring to bear unwanted scrutiny."

Matt stole a glance at John. "Put me down to cover a shift or two after we get past the wedding." He put a hand on his cousin's shoulder. "Don't worry, nothing will interfere with tomorrow. We won't allow it. Come on, let's go back to the house and get ready for dinner at the club. It could prove interesting." He remembered the two pieces of hay in his pocket and plucked them out and passed them to John. "Here, hold these. Dad, you pick. You know which is which, right?"

Earl reached out and plucked one of the pieces of straw from John's hand. Matt took the other and held it up in triumph.

~~~

Sandra stared around the room in awe. She had heard about the Elkford Country Club, but she never thought about seeing the inside of it. Even when she became engaged to John, it never crossed her mind she would attend functions within the hallowed walls, much less be the guest of honor, along with John, at a dinner there.

At least they dined in a private room adjoining the main dining area. Even then, people popped in to speak to Kathryn Stuart. Almost everyone seemed to feel they needed to do so, a constant parade of Elkford society and that of Bruce County, Wallace County, and possibly other nearby locales lacking sufficient numbers of wealthy families to support their own country club.

John slipped his left hand over her right, and she relaxed a little. She knew he didn't care for this part of being a Stuart. He rarely came to the club unless he was staying at his mother's and she and Winston planned to dine there. Since their engagement, he had remained at Kathryn's except for one night early on, and Kathryn rarely suffered the company of the club. Those members whom she liked and respected she saw elsewhere. The rest she avoided, or more likely they avoided crossing paths with her.

When a man in his middle thirties walked into the room tugging a woman of about twenty behind him, Sandra felt John's fingers tighten on her hand. The man greeted Jeanette and Winston at the far end of the room before moving along toward Kathryn, who sat to John's right.

"Hello, Mrs. Stuart. It's so nice to see you here at our club." He extended his hand toward her, but she made no effort to meet him halfway.

"Mr. Michaelson," she said with a nod. "I take it this is your new wife?"

"Yes." He all but snatched the young woman forward. "Lilly, this is Mrs. Stuart. You've heard me mention her."

This time, Kathryn reached out and took the girl's offered hand. "We met when you were quite young. Your father and my late husband had some business dealings during the war. Alistair was pleased with the arrangement. He thought highly of the quality of work your father's company produced and the integrity he showed in all their business dealings."

Vaughn pulled Lilly back to take control of the conversation again. With a smirking look at Sandra, he said, "Lilly has recently given me most pleasurable news. She is to bless me with another child next year. She has already proven to be a good mother to my two sons by my late wife. I'm sure she'll do an admirable job with her own. Perhaps she and the new Mrs. Stuart will cross paths. I believe they share the same doctor. Perhaps our children will be good friends in the future."

Sandra blushed all the way to the roots of her blond curls. At six months, there was no hiding the fact she was with child, though few outside family and friends had been so bold as to allude to the fact in her presence.

"Mr. Michaelson," Kathryn snapped, "while we appreciate you and your wife coming here to wish John and Sandra well in their future together, for I assume that is your intent though you have yet to do so, we are about to present gifts and have our dessert so we may leave. We have a great deal to do tomorrow and require an early start. If you will excuse us, we will get on with our *private* gathering."

His lips compressed into a straight line, but he bowed and tugged Lilly toward the door. "Of course, Mrs. Stuart. However, I still wish to discuss some club business with you in the future. Please have your secretary arrange a time at your convenience, though with the tremendous loss you suffered this week, I understand it may be some time before you're free to discuss the club." He disappeared out the door, Lilly hurrying behind.

Sandra shook herself and tried to focus on John. "I'm sorry, what did you say?"

"I said he's even sleazier than I remembered," John whispered.

She nodded. "He's right, you know. I saw his wife in the waiting room at the doctor's office. I wonder if it's too late to switch back to that odious doctor in Woodbury. I hope he never accompanies her to an appointment. I'd hate to know he's in the waiting room while I'm in the back getting examined."

"I'm glad you never go without your mother. If she ever can't go with you, I'll go."

Sandra just nodded again.

"Do not let him bother you, dear," Kathryn said. "He's trying to bait us. We cannot allow that to happen. Push him out of your mind and focus on tomorrow. You officially become a Stuart in about sixteen hours. Unfortunately, dealing with such people is one of the consequences, but those instances are rare." Kathryn reached across to squeeze Sandra's hand. "Now, we have gifts to present. Let us proceed with the pleasantness we intended for tonight."

Chapter 21

Friday, December 23, 1955

Sandra put her hand on her swollen belly, rubbing it slowly. The baby shifted in response. Not a sound could be heard in the Duncan cottage. She wondered how Greg fared sleeping on the sofa. She hated to displace him, but she wanted to spend one last night in her family home. She and Cindy sat up late talking like they had so often until her sister left after marrying Calvin. Greg swore he fit just fine on the sofa, allowing Sandra to sleep in his room while Cindy and Cal slept in the room the girls shared for six years. Hopefully Greg slept well.

She reached for the windup clock beside the bed. The glowing hands showed it to be quarter before six. Millie's alarm always went off at six o'clock. Today would be no different. She suspected her mother was lying awake, too. Sandra replaced the clock on the bedside table and switched on the lamp.

Across the room hung her wedding dress, smuggled out of the house so John wouldn't accidentally see it after her last fitting on Tuesday night. She lay back on the bed studying it, imagining the look on John's face when she stepped into the sanctuary on Greg's arm in a few hours. The baby moved again, impatient to begin the day. A further shift planted it firmly atop her bladder.

"All right, little one. I'm getting up."

~~~

When John walked into the dining room, Kathryn, Matt, and Earl were already well into their breakfast. "Have any of you looked outside? It's going to be a beautiful, clear day. I don't think it's as cold this morning either. Sure not like it was early in the week."

Swallowing a bite of toast, Matt turned to his father. "I don't think he'd notice if tornadoes were ripping through the cove and reindeer were falling from the sky. Did you notice his glassy eyes?"

Earl snickered. "Just you wait, Matt. One day it will be you about to marry the woman of your dreams. Give him a break today. I heard him on the steps, so at least he didn't float downstairs."

Ignoring the male contingent, John kissed his grandmother's cheek. "Good morning, Gramma. Are you sure you'll be all right putting up with just Matt and Uncle Earl in the house once Sandra and I move next door?"

Her eyebrows arched upward. "I've been putting up with Matt and you together in this house for some time. It's no better or worse." She patted his cheek before asking, "Did you sleep well, dear? It will be a long day."

"Yes, ma'am." He grabbed a plate and began to fill it from the buffet. "Do you think we should call the Duncans to make sure they don't have any issues with the cold?"

Earl leaned toward his son and whispered, "Didn't he just brag about how nice the weather is this morning compared to earlier in the week?"

"Yes," Matt replied in a loud whisper. "We may need to get him evaluated this morning to ensure he's capable of making major life decisions. Shall I call Sandra and warn her, or should that come from you or Aunt Kate?"

John held up a biscuit from the buffet and gripped it like a fastball. A quick glance at Kathryn to catch her eye was followed by a grin at Matt. "I would, but Lila has enough to do today without sweeping the dining room."

"Lila wouldn't be the one sweeping the dining room, young man," the cook said from the door. "Just because you're eighteen and about to marry in a few hours doesn't mean I won't take a broom to you or your scamp cousin...or his father should any of you mess up my spotless floor before handing it to you to use to clean up your mess."

John dropped the biscuit onto his plate and put an arm around Lila's shoulders. "I promise I wouldn't really throw it at him, Lila. You'll have to wait until the next generation to worry about food flying in here."

"I'll make an exception for the little one when the time comes, but I better not catch you three causing me extra work. Especially not today. I've got a horde of people to feed this afternoon. Finish your breakfast and stay out of my kitchen." She retreated into her domain, muttering as she went, "I hope you and Miss Sandra have a sweet little baby girl. Too many roughhousing boys in this family."

~~~

"All right, Greg, you're driving my car. I don't want to risk getting my shoes scuffed driving today. Go ahead and get it warmed up. Cal already has his warming." Millie rushed down the hall to check on her daughters, stealing a look at her watch. Eleven-oh-five. They needed to leave for the church.

Cindy stepped out of the bedroom. "We're ready, Mother." She turned and beckoned to her sister. "Come on. Your groom is probably more nervous than Mother."

Sandra followed her sister into the hall. "I'm coming. Are the bouquets already in the car?"

Millie reached out and took each of her daughters' hands. "You look beautiful, Sandra. You, too, Cindy. Yes, the bouquets are in the trunk of Cal's car nice and safe. Greg just went out to start my car, so it will be warm in a few minutes."

Cindy reached out and took Sandra's free hand with her own. "I'm so pleased things have worked out, Sandra. You and John went through a lot to get here." She squeezed her sister's and Mother's hands before releasing both. "I'll ride with Greg. Mother, you ride in the back of our car with Sandra."

Millie tightened her grip on her younger daughter's hand and led her down the hall behind Cindy. "Are you very nervous, dear?"

"No, not at all, Mother. I'll finally be John's wife in a little more than an hour. I can't wait." She stopped, causing Millie to turn and look back. "Thank you, Mother, for all your support. I know things didn't happen in the right order and it's awfully early to get married and have a baby, but we'll make it because you and Grandmother Kathryn and a lot of other people have helped us. We won't ever forget that. I love you, Mother."

"I love you, too, darling." Tears pooled in both mother's and daughter's eyes. "I'd hug you if it wouldn't wrinkle your dress. I'll make up for it later though." She pulled a handkerchief from her purse and dabbed at Sandra's eyes and then her own. "We better not start crying or Cindy will fuss about us ruining our makeup."

"Come on," Sandra said, tugging on Millie's hand. "Let's go get me married."

~~~

"Stop pacing, John. She'll be here soon. If you aren't careful, you'll wear a hole in the bottom of your shoes. Then the best man will have to drive back to the house to get you another pair, and you don't have another that nice to wear with your suit." Matt patted his pockets for something to use to distract John.

"What if they had a problem with Cal's car? We should have sent Uncle Earl to get them in Gramma's." The groom reached one end of the small room and snapped around to pace the opposite direction.

"John, it will be fine," Kathryn replied. "If they have an issue with one car, the other will come ahead and we'll send Earl back with mine if necessary. They just drove hundreds of miles in Cal's car earlier this week. It should be in fine shape. Besides, I assure you the reverend will not try to start the ceremony until the bride arrives, and she isn't due for another five minutes. She's only to get here early enough for Millie and Cindy to check her gown."

A shadow fell across the room, and John turned his attention to the door hoping to see Greg or Cal. However, it was his mother who stood in the entrance.

"I hardly think you need worry, John," Jeanette said. She moved into the room, ignoring Matt and Kathryn. "There is no way that girl won't show up this morning to claim her prize." She pinched her lips tight, stopping in front of her son. She adjusted his tie and boutonniere. "You look quite handsome, John. I do wish you well even though the choice you have made is not what I wanted for you."

He brushed his lips against her cheek. "Thank you, Mother. I appreciate that."

"Are Winston and I still allowed to sit on the front row as a part of the groom's family?"

"Of course, Mother, just as you rehearsed it yesterday. You, Winston, Gramma, and Uncle Earl will be on the front row on my side."

Someone cleared his throat, and John noticed the minister in the doorway. "The bride and her party have arrived. It's time for those of you not a part of the ceremony to be seated. Mrs. Stuart, Mrs. Hathaway, if you'll proceed to the sanctuary door to be escorted to your seats?"

Matt stood from where he had been leaning against a window. "I'll be right back, Reverend. I need to escort Aunt Kate." In *sotto voce*, he added, "Dad drew the short straw."

~~~

The organist began the last piece before the bridal processional, and Matt held out his arm to Kathryn. They walked down the aisle, Kathryn silently acknowledging friends along the way. Earl followed with Jeanette on his arm and Winston trailing them. Kathryn took the seat next to the aisle. When Jeanette arrived, she glared at the slight but took the spot next to her former mother-in-law. Winston sat next to his wife, and Earl continued onward to take the seat beside Winston. Matt stole a quick look at the foursome before disappearing through the side door where John and the minister waited.

Kathryn leaned her head close to Jeanette's and whispered, "You know what will happen if you disrupt this wedding in any way?"

Through clenched teeth, Jeanette hissed, "Yes."

Satisfied, Kathryn turned her attention to the side door.

The minister entered, and John and Matt followed him. They took their places, and Mary hurried up the side aisle and slipped into her seat next to her mother and Jonah immediately behind the Stuart family.

Calvin entered with Millie on his arm, and the mother of the bride took her place on the front row opposite Kathryn. Vance was seated in the row behind her, and she favored him with a brief smile. Cal sat beside her just as the organist completed the music.

Gwen, stationed at the rear, signaled all was ready, and the organist began the processional. Cindy entered, smiling at the crowd which had turned out to see her sister marry the man she loved. She winked at John and Matt when she took her place opposite them.

Millie stood and stepped just far enough out to ensure a good view when Sandra entered the sanctuary. The rest of the congregation stood with her.

Greg stepped forward, his sister on his arm. He resisted urges both to tug at his collar and to race down the aisle.

Sandra forgot the circumstances which had forced her early marriage and all the problems thrown at her and John over the last few months, focusing only on his smile as he waited for her at the far end of the room.

John stood breathless at the sight of his bride, glowing in her beautiful wedding gown. He watched her float toward him, almost oblivious to everything else. He barely heard Greg answer the minister's query about who gave the bride away, focused only on her hand being placed in his.

Neither bride nor groom noticed when the minister reached the line asking if anyone objected to the union, though Jeanette heard it clearly. Sandwiched among her landlord, her husband, both Hunters, Lila, Mary, and Jonah, she kept her lips carefully sealed, though her insides seethed.

In minutes, it was over. John carefully folded back the veil with Cindy's help and claimed his first kiss from his wife. She slipped her arm through his, and the beaming couple hurried down the aisle. Matt held out his arm for Cindy, and Millie followed them, escorted on each side by Greg and Cal. Earl bypassed Jeanette this time to extend his arm to Kathryn. They followed the bride's family, leaving Winston to bring his wife along.

~~~

"Dad and I have shed our coats and ties. Why are you still wearing both?" Matt reached out and gave John's tie a tug.

"If I have to wear this dress until the end, he can wear the coat and tie," Sandra responded for her new husband before leaning up for the hundredth kiss since the one at the altar.

"You could both change into something more comfortable. The crowd is mostly gone now. Nobody left but family and a few close friends. They wouldn't care."

"No, we're fine. It isn't dark yet, is it?" Sandra hadn't had time to even look out the window since they returned to the mansion for the reception.

"No, but it won't be long."

"All right, then we need to get ready to leave. We want to do that before it gets dark." She looked around, trying to locate her mother.

"Sandra, you're only walking across to the carriage house. It isn't a hundred feet."

"Yes," John finally chimed in, "but we want to go over there for the night before it gets completely dark. Oh, I need to go up and get my shaving kit and a couple of other things."

"Already taken care of. Dad snuck up and got those together earlier. He and Cindy took your bag and Sandra's over already. You're all set."

"Oh, good. Thanks, Matt, for everything you and your dad have done for us."

"Yes, Matt, we appreciate all you've done. We need to speak to Uncle Earl, too, to thank him personally, John."

"Don't worry, he'll be here for another two days. We will see you two this weekend, right? I mean, other than for Sunday services on Christmas?" Matt grinned at his cousins.

"Yes, Matt," Sandra said with an exaggerated sigh. "There's no food in the carriage house yet except juice and coffee and eggs and grits and bacon and white bread. John will have to come over here if he wants biscuits for breakfast until I get better at making them. We'll see you for dinner tomorrow if not before."

"Good. It will be strange to be here without the two of you after all these months. Once Dad leaves, it will be quiet in the evenings. Of course, Aunt Kate and I will go back to trying to outmaneuver one another at chess like we used to when John stayed at his mother's house." He drummed his fingers on his chin. "I need to find the score sheet. I can't remember who's ahead on wins."

~~~

The remaining guests, all family or staff, lined a path from the mansion to the carriage house. The bride and groom emerged and stopped atop the stairs to acknowledge the cheers of those nearest and dearest to them. To Sandra's surprise, John scooped her up into his arms before trotting down the steps. As he made his way across to their new home, rice pelted them from all sides.

Matt stood beside the small door leading into the carriage house. He gave the couple a quick hug before dousing them with a handful of rice and closing the door behind them.

John stopped at the bottom of the stairs to claim their first private kiss as husband and wife. A quick check assured him the door at the top stood open, something else Matt and Earl thought about ahead of time for the happy couple. He climbed the steps, stopping at the threshold to claim another kiss before stepping across into their apartment.

When he set her on her feet at last, she kept her arms wrapped around his neck, extending their kisses for several minutes. Their lips parted at last, and Sandra smiled up at her new husband.

"I can't believe we're finally married. After everything we went through, we made it." She popped up on her toes for another quick peck on his lips. "Why don't I go take off this dress and put on something comfortable? I'd like nothing more than for us to sit on the sofa and relax right now. Is that all right with you?"

"Perfect. It's been a long day. Sitting and relaxing sounds pretty good for now." John bent to steal another kiss. "We can get around to other things later."

She grinned again. "Finally without worrying about anyone catching us. I'm so glad Grandmother Kathryn offered us this apartment. I sure wouldn't want to spend the night with her or Matt or Uncle Earl in the next room. I suppose we'll get used to that idea eventually, but no time soon."

She disappeared into their bedroom, and John slid off his coat and tugged loose his tie. He kicked off his shoes and hung the coat and tie over the back of one of the four chairs around their small dining table.

"Want me to light a fire in the fireplace?" he called.

"That would be nice," Sandra answered from the bedroom. "We can sit in front of it with the lights off. Have you tested the radio yet? I hope it can pick up one or two stations in Woodbury as well as the one in Elkford. Maybe even some of the clear channel stations?"

"I'll set it on the local one for now. I tested that a couple of days ago. We can search for others later." He turned on the radio and began to arrange the paper, wood, and coal in the grate.

Sandra came out, dressed in warm sweater and wool slacks. "I'll hang up your coat." She took it and disappeared again. When she returned, John had lit the paper and stood watching it. Sandra stole up behind him and slipped her arms around his waist. "Looks perfect. Come on, let's sit and watch it."

They settled on the sofa, and Sandra snuggled close to him, her head on his shoulder and her arms still draped around his waist. John placed one arm across her shoulders. His other hand found her swollen belly and rubbed it slowly. As the paper and wood burned away, the light in the room dwindled, leaving only the red glow of the coal in the fireplace.

Chapter 22

Monday, March 19, 1956

"I can't believe Mr. Hutchins gave us so many problems to work on our first day back to school after spring holidays." John opened the rear door of the new 1956 blue and white Ford Fordor and dropped his books on the seat before climbing into the front.

Sliding into the passenger side of the car, Matt set his books on the floor under his feet before answering. "It isn't that many. They're straightforward, so we can knock them out in less than half an hour. It will take longer to read those two stories for English and write up something about the main characters' motivations." He spotted a grain of rice tucked into the seatbelt's fold and plucked it out. "I think we overdid it on showering Jonah and Mary with rice. It was nice of you to let them use your car for their honeymoon."

Jonah and Mary had married the previous week, and someone had hit Jonah's truck days before the wedding. The newlyweds only had a long weekend to celebrate before Jonah started a big project for a new customer, and John and Sandra insisted they take the new Ford for the short honeymoon while the truck got repaired. Rice caught in Mary's veil and dress had shown up in various places ever since despite her best efforts to get it all out.

John started the car and backed out when the traffic behind him cleared. As he shifted into first and began to move forward, Matt noticed movement to his right and exclaimed, "What's gotten into the principal's secretary? Look at her running around. I've never seen her so animated."

Following Matt's direction, John spotted the woman just as she stopped where some of their friends congregated on the sidewalk. Perry, one of the boys in the group, whirled around and began searching the parking lot. When he saw John's car, he broke into a run toward it.

"Now what?" John mumbled, bringing the Ford to a stop. "I need to get home to Sandra."

"It won't take but a minute to find out," Matt said. He cranked down his window in time for Perry to almost slam into the side of the car, breathless from the run.

"John," Perry gasped, "your grandmother just called the office. You need to go to the hospital."

"What's wrong? Did she say? Is something wrong with Sandra?" A car horn blasted from behind them where traffic had begun to collect.

"The baby is coming!" Perry jumped clear when John released the clutch and the car shot forward.

"Hey, Perry, Greg's at baseball practice. Let him know," Matt called as John sped away, weaving around cars in the parking lot to find the quickest exit. "John, you realize we'll probably beat them to the hospital by ten minutes or more unless something slowed Aunt Kate in calling the school." He cranked his window up to shut out the cold breeze whipping into the vehicle.

"Maybe so, but I don't want her wondering where I am if they left earlier and are already at the hospital." A Chevy let him into the line near the entrance, and he honked at the front car when it didn't pull into traffic fast enough to suit him. "Her due date isn't until next week, Matt. What if something's wrong? Maybe something happened that Gramma didn't want to say on the phone, like Sandra got sick or fell or..."

"John, I don't know much about babies or when they appear, but I know those due dates aren't exact. Heck, I've been told I didn't show up for more than a week after I was supposed to be born. I'm sure everything is–" Matt swallowed his words when John hit the gas to squeeze into a tiny gap in traffic and dart onto the main road. "John, we don't need to become patients at the hospital. That would make it harder for you to ensure Sandra's OK."

John forced himself to relax his grip on the wheel and eased off the accelerator. "I know. I can't help it, Matt. I'll feel much better when this is over, and the baby is here, and they're both out of the hospital."

Chuckling, Matt said, "You mean when you're getting almost no sleep because the baby is crying to be fed every couple of hours during the night and you're worried about that and Sandra not getting enough rest and you taking a math test the next morning?" Matt looked in the backseat where John's formerly neat stack of books lay scattered after his harrowing exit from the parking lot. "Shall we work on those math problems while we wait for the doctor to tell you if you have a boy or a girl?"

John finally smiled. "Somehow I don't think I'll be at school tomorrow, so I won't worry about those or that reading assignment."

~~~

Per Matt's expectation, he and John arrived at the Bruce County Hospital in Elkford before Sandra and Millie. When Vance's car pulled up to the entrance, the boys stood waiting. John opened the back door and quizzed Sandra about her condition before helping her stand and move to a wheelchair a nurse had ready. Millie followed, and the group proceeded into the hospital while Vance parked in a nearby space.

When a delay approaching twenty seconds kept Sandra waiting to be assigned a room, Matt had to outmaneuver John to keep him from irritating the frazzled admissions clerk. A conveniently timed contraction helped shift John's focus to Sandra, allowing Millie to handle the details at the desk. Once things were set to right, the group followed the nurse pushing Sandra to the elevator.

After the mother-to-be was settled in her third-floor room, Matt walked to the other end of the hall to a payphone to report to Kathryn. "Room 328. They said the doctor is here, but he's delivering another baby. When they ran me out of the room, the nurse was to check Sandra over and report to him. They expect him to be done with the one he's delivering any time, so Sandra should get his full attention soon."

"I doubt there is any reason to hurry," the elderly matron said. "These things generally take time, though one can never be sure. His nurses are quite competent. They know when to summon him."

"Do you want me to drive up there in John's car and bring you to the hospital, Aunt Kate? Or is someone there who can drive you into Elkford?"

"No, dear, I told Millie and Sandra I will remain here and await word this evening. I am a little old to sit all night at the hospital. Jonah will be home soon. Would you like me to ask him to pick you up and bring you here to retrieve your own car? I expect you will wish to remain there to support John, but you still have schoolwork to consider. I would not have you let your grades slip so near graduation."

"I can do my homework while I sit in the waiting room. I hope to get John to do some of his so I can turn it in for him tomorrow though he'll miss school. Do you think this could go on all night?"

"Oh my, dear, it could take until tomorrow sometime, though I hope that will not be the case."

Matt watched a frustrated John get pushed out of Sandra's room by a nurse. "Hmmm, maybe having my car available wouldn't be a bad idea. John might need his here, so I hate to borrow it later tonight or to go to school tomorrow. I could get a buddy to pick me up from here for school, but I don't have a change of clothes."

"Give me the telephone number of the payphone. I will ask Jonah to call you to discuss what arrangements make the most sense. The two of you may sort out those details."

"That's a good idea, Aunt Kate." He read off the number of the payphone. "I should be close enough to hear it when it rings." He watched John pacing back and forth in front of Sandra's closed door with a mixture of amusement and sympathy. "They've kicked John out of the room now. I better go distract him until they let him back in."

"All right, Matt. Update me with any news, and tell Millie to call if she needs anything. I shall visit in the morning unless my presence is required before that time."

"Yes, Aunt Kate, I will. I'll talk to you later this evening. Goodbye."

~~~

John threw up his hands in frustration. "I can't concentrate on calculus problems." He shoved his book onto the adjacent table and dropped his pencil on top of it. "I wish they would stop making me come out here while they check on Sandra. I've spent the last three hours going back and forth between the waiting room and Sandra's room. Why won't the baby decide it's time to be born? Can't the doctor do something to speed things along?"

Matt set aside his literature book, careful to mark his place first. He had long since finished his calculus problems. "Why don't we go get something to eat in the cafeteria while you've been banished from Sandra's room again? Her mother is with her. If we don't eat soon, they'll close for the night, and I don't think Lila will offer to bring something down here for us to eat."

John shook his head. "No, neither do I." He looked over at Matt. "You know, you can go home and have some of Lila's cooking for dinner. You don't need to stay here all night. Jonah and Mary brought your car down. Why don't you go get dinner and a good night's sleep?"

"I might go home later, but I'm not leaving you yet to sit out in the waiting room alone every time they kick you out but let Millie stay with Sandra. You know, that isn't fair. We should complain about such treatment."

As if to agree with Matt's dinner suggestion, John's stomach chose that moment to rumble. He sighed and stood. "I guess I do need to eat something. Sandra got on me earlier about not eating, and the doctor said the baby isn't quite ready to come yet. Let's bring it back up here to eat though. I don't want to be gone too long. Let me tell Millie we're going downstairs." Matt hopped up to follow, but a familiar voice stopped both young men in their tracks.

"This way, Winston." Jeanette appeared at the far end of the hall, her husband in tow. "There he is." She pointed at her son, who stood a few steps from Sandra's door. "John, dear, I must speak to you."

Rubbing his temple with one hand, John whispered, "Go ahead to the cafeteria without me. I don't want you to miss dinner."

With a nod, Matt replied, "I'll bring you back a selection of what looks good." As he passed Jeanette and Winston, he smiled broadly. "Good of you to come support John for the birth of his child, Jeanette. I know he'll appreciate it. So will Aunt Kate."

At the mention of her landlord, Jeanette slowed. "I always support my son. I think of him first at all times."

Before either could continue, John caught up to them, prompting Matt not to stop to antagonize her further. "Hello, Mother. Thank you for coming. Sandra will be pleased, too. You can go in to see her in a few minutes. The doctor is in with her now. He said it would probably be some time before the baby arrives, but I expect you know that since you've been through this."

She stole a look behind her where Matt disappeared into the elevator before answering. "Yes, it can take hours, especially with a first child."

The door to Sandra's room opened, and her doctor and mother exited. Millie spotted John, Jeanette, and Winston and walked over to speak to her counterpart. "Hello, Jeanette, Winston. Would you like to see Sandra for a moment? Her contractions are about eight minutes apart, so the doctor plans to leave her in her room."

Her eyes darting around, Jeanette stammered, "Uh, no, I should not like to disturb her. She should rest as much as possible. I expect it will be a long night."

"Yes, you're probably right." Millie looked around the hallway. "Where's Matt? Did you convince him to go home, John?"

"The cafeteria. We were about to get something to eat and bring it back here. I was going to knock on the door to let you know when Mother and Winston appeared, so Matt went ahead to get something for us." He turned back to his mother. "I should have asked if you and Winston wanted anything, Mother. Colonel Waters is bringing Millie something when he returns from picking up Greg from a friend's house, but..."

Waving him off, Jeanette said, "No, no, we dined early at the club. I expected it to take some time this evening, so we went there to eat after we received your call." She put her hand on his arm and leaned closer. "You could go there and have something better than the fare from the hospital cafeteria. There is no call for you to wait here for hours."

John pressed his lips together. "No, Mother, I intend to stay here until the baby is born. I would not consider abandoning Sandra to dine at the country club when she is in labor."

"Really, John, I accept you did what you thought was the right thing by the girl, but there is no cause to allow your health or your schoolwork to suffer waiting for this child to be born."

John struggled to control his voice, but it seethed with anger. "Mother, I will be here when my wife gives birth to my child. Thank you for stopping by to show your support."

When Matt returned ten minutes later, he found a scowling John and Millie in Sandra's room but no sign of Jeanette or Winston. By the time Vance arrived with dinner for Millie fifteen minutes later, the mood in the room had returned to the normal excited expectation of the pending birth.

~~~

Squeaking roused the members of the Stuart party in the maternity ward waiting room. A gurney wheeled into view with a nurse scurrying along beside it. When a familiar form followed, Matt's eyes popped fully open. A quick glance at his watch told him it was after midnight. They still waited for the doctor to decide Sandra was close enough to giving birth to be sent to the delivery room.

Matt turned his attention to the newcomer. The attendant had pushed the gurney into a room two away from Sandra's. The nurse closed the door in the man's face. Matt eyed him, wondering if he would backtrack to the waiting area and notice the other occupants. John and Millie remained in Sandra's room, leaving Greg and Vance as the only other occupants outside. Vaughn Michaelson wouldn't be likely to know either of them, but he might recognize Matt. They had crossed paths a few times when Kathryn took the boys to some function at the country club.

Not willing to sit idly by, Matt stood when Vaughn walked toward the waiting area. Vaughn's reaction answered the question. "Hello, Matt, isn't it? Mrs. Stuart's ward or something?"

"Great nephew, Mr. Michaelson. Was that your wife they brought up here? I hope she doesn't have any serious problem."

"Lilly? No, she fell at home and got a couple of bumps. Just a minor accident. She's clumsy that way. Since she's with child, I insisted they keep her overnight at least. Can't be too careful with one of my heirs." He sat down and motioned for Matt to do the same, like the man was in his private office. "What brings you here so late? Not somewhere I'd expect a young buck like you to choose for a hangout," he said with a snicker.

Matt, who remained standing, said, "John's wife is here. There will be a new Stuart heir in the next few hours."

"That so? Seems we'll have a Michaelson heir and a Stuart heir coming along close together. Lilly should present my next in a few months. They'll start school together. I'll be watching to see my son up against the Stuart's." The door to Lilly Michaelson's room opened. The nurse gestured to Vaughn to come in, and he rose. "I look forward to seeing the new Stuart prince tomorrow when I come to fetch Lilly home. If they failed and get stuck with a girl this time...well, they can always try again." He snickered once more before he ambled off to see his wife.

No sooner had Vaughn shut his wife's door than John popped out of Sandra's room. "It's time. They're about to move her down the hall to delivery." The same attendant passed John. Less than a minute later, they wheeled Sandra out on the gurney, Millie walking along on one side holding the girl's hand. John took up position on the other and did likewise. Matt, Vance, and Greg fell into line behind.

When they pushed Sandra through the double doors into the delivery area, a nurse pointed toward another waiting room. John stood rooted in place until Millie and Matt dragged him over to the chair nearest the doors.

"Hey," Matt said, "guess who I saw just before you came out? Vaughn Michaelson. His wife was admitted. He said she fell, and he wanted her here overnight. What are the odds of them being here tonight?"

"Pretty long, I'd say," John responded. He looked down at his watch.

Millie placed her hand on his arm. "John, it will be more than fifteen minutes. It's progressed enough the doctor felt it time to move her to the delivery room, but it could still be several hours. Try to relax."

"Yeah, you need to be able to function when the doctor comes out to tell you the baby's finally here," Matt added. He sat down next to John. Vaughn's presence hadn't fazed the expectant father. Matt would need to think of something else to distract him. "Hey, have you and Sandra written up anything for the newspaper yet? You can't give the baby's name or anything about it until it's here and you know if it's a boy or girl, but the other stuff they put in those announcements can be ready." He pulled a small notepad from his shirt pocket. "We could work on that. Your name and Sandra's and Millie's and your mother and Aunt Kate and of course me as godfather. I don't want this to be delayed getting into the Sunday newspaper. I'll need to send copies around like I did for your wedding announcement."

That reminder got John's attention. "Like to Claudine? Mother still fumes about you sending a copy of the wedding announcement to that crazy girl. Winston got an earful from her mother's father. Claudine must have thrown things all over the house when she got it."

"I'll check my list to see if she's included." He grinned at John. "I know Dad's on it. I'm not sure who else. However, I can't imagine Claudine not wanting to know she has a little step nephew or niece. She's probably already plotting to marry her firstborn to yours to unite the families."

John shuddered. "What a horrible thought."

"Could be worse. Vaughn Michaelson will have a child just a few months younger than yours."

John stared at Matt, openmouthed. "I wish I knew which would be worse."

~~~

At almost three o'clock in the morning, the doctor walked into the waiting room. John jumped up. Millie sprang to her feet almost as quickly, and Vance rose with her. Roused by the sudden movement, Matt and Greg woke and sat up.

"Mr. Stuart, you have a healthy baby girl. Mrs. Stuart is well, also."

Shaking the doctor's hand, John said, "Thank you. May I see them?"

"Yes, you and Mrs. Duncan may go in to see them for a moment. Then Mrs. Stuart will be taken to her room and the baby to the nursery." He patted John's shoulder and walked back toward the delivery area.

John took Millie's hand, and they hurried after the doctor. When the nurse at the door admitted them, they separated, going to opposite sides of the gurney Sandra rested on. The nurses had her propped up, and she held a tiny bundle encased in a cream blanket.

Leaning down to kiss his wife, John whispered, "I love you, Sandra. How are you feeling?"

"Mmm, tired and sore, but not too bad. I think I'll feel much better once I've eaten something and taken a nap, but for now I just want to hold her."

Millie pulled the blanket back to better see her granddaughter's face. The baby yawned and stretched, one little fist upraised. "I believe she has a bit of red tint to that blond hair. Mrs. Stuart will be pleased. What color are her eyes?"

"Blue, but she said John's and his father's started blue and changed to hazel later. I think hers might, too." Sandra grinned up at her husband. "That should end any debate on her name, John. At least her first name."

"We agreed each side would be recognized if we chose that route. Do you still like what we discussed?"

"Yes, I do. Agreed?"

He stroked one of the baby's soft, rosy cheeks with a finger. "Kathryn Duncan Stuart. Kathryn for my grandmother for all the support she's provided; Duncan for your family for the same reason since your mother," he looked up at Millie, "declined to have the baby named for her. Are you sure, Millie?"

"Yes, I'm sure. Kathryn Duncan Stuart. I like that."

Epilogue

Friday, June 1, 1956

Matt burst through the front door of Chestnut Cove waving his diploma. "Told you they would still give it to me, Dad."

Earl Hunter followed his son, tugging at his tie to loosen it. "Who in their right mind gave you a platform to stand up and speak in front of your class, teachers, and all those guests?" The same twitch so common at the corner of Matt's mouth tugged at his father's. "It isn't like you don't get enough talking done without them handing you a captive audience. I would have hated for you to say something to cause them to withhold your diploma at the last minute. Your entry into Coughton Tech might have been in jeopardy."

Newlyweds Mary and Jonah followed Earl and Matt, Mary hurrying toward the kitchen to help her mother. Lila had declined to attend graduation, preferring instead to prepare the celebratory dinner to follow.

Kathryn, Millie, Greg, and Vance trailed them and joined Earl, Matt, and Jonah in the great room. When Sandra and John failed to appear after several minutes, the newly crowned Elkford High School valedictorian asked Kathryn, "Did Jeanette say they would join us for dinner tonight, Aunt Kate?"

Kathryn's eyes closed a moment. "She indicated they would do so. I reminded her I would not tolerate any disparaging remarks about Sandra or little KD. My sources inform me she has made them on several occasions at the country club and at church. I regret Reverend Walker is no longer pastor there. While he disappointed me with regard to the wedding, he did not tolerate wicked gossip and would have said something to restrain her tongue at least on Sundays. I hope he finds success at his new church in Woodbury."

"Calling her own granddaughter a bastard should get her kicked out of church," Matt grumbled.

They heard the front door open and close, followed by slow taps down the half-dozen stairs. Sandra appeared a moment later carrying her child in one arm with her purse and diaper bag slung over the opposite shoulder. "Mr. and Mrs. Hathaway are here. They're talking to John outside. They should be inside in a moment."

Matt beat Millie to the young mother. "Let me take something, Sandra." Instead of the baggage, he scooped the baby from her arm. "Come to Uncle Matty, KD. I haven't held my goddaughter all day." He tucked her into one arm like he had been taught and began to babble to her, hoping to elicit a giggle.

The front door could be heard opening again. John appeared around the corner moments later. He stole a glance at his grandmother and shook his head. The others understood his meaning: they would be spared Jeanette and Winston's presence at dinner.

<center>~~~</center>

After a peaceful if boisterous meal, Kathryn stood from her place at the head of the table. "It has been an eventful last year. I am delighted to have welcomed two new additions to the Stuart family. Sandra and little KD have brought a brightness long absent from Chestnut Cove. I am also pleased for Millie and the rest of the Duncans to be a part of my extended family." Her eyes twinkled when she added, "Perhaps that family shall also expand in the near future."

Vance and Millie both blushed. Their growing attachment had blossomed into romance once the hectic period surrounding John and Sandra's wedding passed.

"While I will miss having John, Sandra, Matt, and KD with me once they leave for Coughton at the end of the summer, I am happy at the direction their lives are moving as John and Matt begin college.

"I am fortunate that Lila and Mary remain with me. I am glad Jonah has joined them next door in the gatehouse and look forward to monitoring his progress growing his construction business." Kathryn's gaze came to rest on Mary. "Now, I believe someone else has an announcement to make?"

At Kathryn's gesture, Mary stood and tugged Jonah up to stand beside her. "We didn't want to overshadow the graduation celebration with our own news, but early next year, KD will have a new playmate."

Sandra hurried around the table to hug her friend, and the young women led the group into the great room. Matt and John went into the kitchen to bring out their graduation cake and ice cream after insisting Lila join the others. They began slicing the cake and scooping the ice cream into bowls and delivering them to their family and friends.

Kathryn rose at last and walked into the great room to where her great-granddaughter lounged watching the festivities from her playpen. "Come, dear. You must join the party." She leaned down and lifted the baby into her arms. "I have much to teach you, KD. I fear I won't live long enough to accomplish it all, but you have two wonderful parents and your Grandmother Millie. I suspect you shall have a Grandfather Vance before long, and you'll have Mary and Jonah and their new baby and Lila. Of course, you'll have your godfather, too. Matt is a fun-loving young man, but he is very shrewd and sharp. He has more to learn from me, but he will serve you well as godfather for years to come. When I am gone, you must listen to him and learn all he will have to teach you, my dear girl."

The End

B. A. Howell is a native of east Alabama. She attended Auburn University followed by a career in engineering in Huntsville and Auburn, Alabama, and Columbus, Georgia, before embarking on the adventure of writing. *Chestnut Cove: Love and Lessons* is her second published novel.

www.ingramcontent.com/pod-product-compliance
Lightning Source LLC
Chambersburg PA
CBHW020404130626
46549CB00006B/2426